Petals of a Three-Leafed Clover

Petals of a Three-Leafed Clover

Julice Howard Franklin

Petals of a Three-Leafed Clover
Copyright, 2015 by Julice Howard Franklin

ISBN: 978-0-578-17037-4

<u>Petals of a Three-Leafed Clover</u>

Published by InstantPublisher
www.instantpublisher.com
Collierville, TN

Edited by Winnie Shields
&
Danita Adams

Cover Design by Velvet Long

Printed in the United States of America

DEDICATED TO

Bertha Howard, Lenora Brown, and four other anonymous persons who loved to recall unusual incidents that actually happened in their lives. Their incredible true stories inspired me to write this story.

CONTENTS

ACKNOWLEDGEMENTS

A sincere thank you to every person who reads this book: Your precious time is very valuable and I thank you.

Thank you to my family, friends, and other special persons. I appreciate all your support and encouragement.

To all readers, librarians, teachers, booksellers and everyone, thank you.

God Bless

Chapter 1

In the beginning

In early Autumn, 1981, a funeral procession made its way slowly through Memphis, on its way to the final resting place for a beautiful young woman many people loved. People stood here and there, watching, as the long fleet of black limos passed. Their hearts were filled with sadness as they watched the white handkerchiefs dab the tears from the eyes of the mourners.

This was a very sorrowful day, but a beautiful day, the day of Yom Kippur. The weather registered a perfect 72 degrees. Autumn leaves falling, bringing to mind for consideration, that everything was all right with God and the Spirit of the deceased was welcomed and all her sins were forgiven.

The funeral procession reached its destination and the long fleet of limousines stopped, and the line of cars proceeded in accordance behind them. Everyone slowly got out of the automobiles to make their way to the gravesite.

As the door to the third limo opened, a beautiful young, ebony skinned woman emerged. She was medium height, thin, with a shapely figure, and legs of a thoroughbred. Her dark tinted glasses covered the sadness in her eyes as she moved along in a proper manner trying to disassociate herself from the crowd.

You could easily discern that her reasons for being there were totally different from the others. Her reasons were for love and true friendship. She and the deceased had an everlasting bond of sisterhood that will always be remembered.

 The young woman was Sarah Anna Foster, confidant and trusted friend to the deceased. Many people referred to her as Ann, or Anna Two, a nickname given to her by a family friend to differentiate her from her grandmother who was also named Sarah Anna Foster.

The day was Thursday, October 8, 1981. The day Virginia Elizabeth Johns-Jamieson was laid to rest. Virginia was "Jenny" to Ann and other friends and loved ones. A loss that left emptiness and hurt in Ann's Spirit that only time will heal.

Ann stood there, at the gravesite, thinking deeply, in silence, trying to bring an acceptable understanding of how Jenny's wonderful life made its way to a pointless end. Ann stood there in a daze, thinking to herself:

"What a beautiful day; beautiful bright sun; a brisk gentle wind blowing against my face. Oh God, what happened to us? How did we get here? Please God, let this be a dream. Shake me and wake me up. Stop it! Stop it! (Ann whispered to herself). I must take hold of myself. I must be strong; strong for the children and for David. Poor, weak, contemptible David, I feel your pain, but I don't feel sorry for you. I hope your pain rip your heart out; you narcissistic son-of-a-bitch! I was disappointed the first time I laid eyes on you. Oh God, help me, please help me, I can't fall apart now. This is not the time. This is Jenny's time. She needs me. I'm here for you Jenny. I'm here for you. Comfort me, Lord. Please comfort me!"

Jenny was the mother of two children. A daughter, Elizabeth Ann Poteice Jamison, called Lizzie, and a son, David Johns Jamieson, called DJ. DJ was named after their father, Jenny's husband, Dr. David Jerrod Jamieson, cum laude graduate,

Meharry Medical College, born, February 12, 1948. He was the only child to an upper class Negro family near Hartford Connecticut. His father was a retired ship builder and his mother was a medical doctor.

David attended predominantly white private schools growing up and got mostly everything any child could want, yet he was never satisfied. His mother hoped sending him to college in the South would help him grow and develop a sense of sensibility for common people. Unfortunately, that didn't work. It only heightened his senseless desires and opened the door for more betrayal and deceit.

Ann tried very hard to like David. She wanted a brotherly relationship with him, but she could never get beyond the intuition that his only purpose was to use people. Everybody loved David and desired his friendship, but Ann never trusted him. She felt he was the cause of Jenny's death and never forgave him for it.

Ann stood quietly, listening to the Holy Orders. Her Spirit was drained, but she believed God would lift her Spirit and move her to tomorrow in peace and end all this hostility. She looked backwards over her shoulder and saw Pot rushing to be by her side. Ann was then reminded of God's promise of comfort and joy. The sight of Pot's face immediately empowered Ann and she was energized with a burst of strength to handle the rest of the day.

Pot found her way to Ann's side. They stood there, shoulder to shoulder, hand in hand, to comfort one another. Even the surroundings of nature knew this was an everlasting friendship at its finest. Ann stood there, hand in hand with Pot, thinking to herself, inspired by Pot's presence.

"Pot is always late. But I knew she would be here. I looked backwards over my shoulder because I could feel her presence. I'm so happy Pot made it."

Ann and Pot, Pottianna Love, stood together, at the resting place of their best friend. Thoughts of their childhood and other life experiences stirred in Ann's mind; moments of how they had been there for one another from childhood to adults. Ann believed in her heart that this was not the end, but a new beginning and Jenny would be with them in Spirit. Ann looked at Pot and smiled; remembering everything about their lives, right from the beginning.

****

I am Sarah Anna Foster, and on a cold, windy Saturday night, December 2, 1950, I was born; the third and last child born to my mother, Amy Mae Foster. And this is my family. My daddy, Charlie Murphy, had disappeared again, for the third time, after getting my mother pregnant. The neighbors said he had gone to Detroit to seek employment in one of the automobile plants. I guess my mother really loved him though, because my grandmother, Mama Sarah, often said my mother never knew any other man and if she did, she never told anybody. The family always laughed about how my mother used to sit alone listening to slow, sad love songs, praying out loud, asking God to please send Charlie Murphy back to her.

We lived in a large home in Memphis, Tennessee, owned by my Aunt Kate. Aunt Kate had run off from her second husband in Mississippi, and moved to Memphis to start a new life. This was a big house, and many family members lived there. The neighbors used to say, *"If you throw a rock on top of the house, children will run out for days."* Yes, we were crowded. Children here and there; some sleeping three and four to a bed; but we were very happy despite our difficulties.

4

Aunt Kate never turned anybody away. If you wanted to leave Mississippi and come to Memphis to start a new life, her door was open to you and your family. All she asked is that you are clean and willing to work. And on December 2, 1950, one more was added to the bunch, me, Sarah Anna Foster, weighing nine pounds and ten ounces, a head full of hair and lungs to wake the dead. I was named after my grandmother whose hands were right there, waiting at the womb, as I made my entrance into this world. Most people call her, Mama Sarah, but most of the time I call her Mama, because that's just what she is to me *"Mama."*

Mama Sarah was born January 2, 1910, the year boxer Jack Johnson floored heavyweight champion Tommy Burns, winning the heavyweight boxing championship of the world. In that same year, the Wright Brothers launched their first commercial airplane flight from Dayton to Columbus, Ohio. Mama Sarah would call this a very good year. Meaning, she would live a long, happy life, filled with the blessings of God forever and ever.

Amy Mae thought I was going to be a Christmas baby, but right after Thanksgiving, when nobody had birthing a baby on their mind, it happened. I was ready and on the way.

On that night, everybody was tired of left-over turkey and it was time for Aunt Kate's after Thanksgiving down home fish fry. The music was loud. Everybody was dancing, doing the jitterbug, and Aunt Kate was frying fish. You could smell the aroma of buffalo fish and hushpuppies two blocks away.

Big Daddy, Aunt Kate's boyfriend, had brought enough beer and whiskey to make all the neighbors drunk. Happiness filled the air. Good food, a good warm fire, soulful music, and a houseful of happy people all in the spirit of the holidays.

Mama Sarah said this was the perfect night for a child like me to be born. She said Amy Mae wasn't her old jovial self that night. She said Amy Mae was moving in slow motion and looked as if she didn't feel too well. Mama said she went over to see about her.

"You hurting child, Mama Sarah asked?"

Mama Sarah could read people like a fortune telling gypsy. She knew when a person was sick, when someone was afraid, happy, and everything else in between. So on that night, Mama Sarah was ready for Ann's entrance into this dimension.

"My stomach doesn't feel too good," Amy Mae answered.

"You ain't in labor are you?"

"No ma'am. It's not time for the baby yet."

"Come on in here," Mama Sarah told her, *"and let me give you a pinch of baking soda, you probably done ate too much fish."*

The moment Amy Mae wobbled from the sofa and stood up, her water broke.

"Shit, baby!" Mama Sarah said to her. *"You are in labor! Hey, y'all,"* Mama Sarah yelled. *"Cut that music down! The baby is coming."*

Everyone there, that night was astonished and amazed. How wonderful! The music got louder. Everybody jumped to their feet dancing and Kate threw more fish in the hot fish grease.

6

Mama Sarah took Amy Mae to her bedroom in the back of the house to prepare for the delivery. She hollered to Kate to bring her doctor's bag and yelled for Louise to put some hot water on the stove.

Mama Sarah knew everything about delivering babies. All the babies in our family were born right at home. Mama Sarah didn't take too kindly to hospitals. She believed many hospitals used Black folk as guinea pigs for medical experiments and it was hard for her to trust them. She believes that all human beings are perfect and the human body heals itself. Mama Sarah believes in the miraculous power of plants and herbs; and, that the fruit of the tree is man's food and the leaves of the tree his medicine. She has a strong love for nature and she believes as Hippocrates believed: *"Let your food be your medicine and your medicine be your food."*

Mama Sarah had six children of her own: my mother, Amy Mae, the youngest; Aunt Kate, the oldest; Aunt Louise; Aunt Bell; Uncle Robert; and Uncle Junior.

Uncle Junior was named after Mama Sarah's husband, their daddy, Benjamin Jack Foster, referred to as Papa Jack. He was killed in the Army in World War II, trying to save a fellow soldier. Uncle Junior was thought to be dead too, but as a child, I never heard the family talk about how he died.

However, many years later, Amy Mae secretly told me that the Pastor of their church in a small Mississippi town was a White man. Amy Mae said our family and many other people believe this White Pastor and his wife kidnapped Uncle Junior. She said Mama Sarah and Papa Jack were very close to them. She said Mama Sarah washed and cleaned for them and was midwife to two of the Pastor's children. They helped each other on their farms, and they planted, and harvested together.

Amy Mae said one year Mama Sarah let Uncle Junior stay with the Pastor for a week to help with their harvest. After that week ended, the Pastor didn't bring Uncle Junior home. Amy Mae said they thought nothing of it though, because that happened all the time. But after that second week passed, Mama Sarah and Papa Jack rode over in the wagon to bring Uncle Junior home. Amy Mae said they thought he was probably a little homesick by then. When they got there, the whole family had moved and there was no sign of Uncle Junior anywhere. Amy Mae said they searched for several days, but Uncle Junior was never found. Neither Uncle Junior nor this family were ever seen or heard of ever again.

Amy Mae said Mama Sara was devastated. She said Mama Sarah got very sick and almost died. She said, from then on, everyone just kept quiet about it, to keep the family from hurting all over again. And me, I kept quiet about it too. I didn't want anything to ever hurt Mama.

Uncle Robert followed in Papa Jack's footsteps and was away in the Army. Aunt Bell had run off to California with Mr. Thurmond Bridgeforth, the lady's husband down the street. Mama Sarah hated her for that. She said Aunt Bell had made the whole family look bad. She said if Aunt Bell ever darkened her door again, she would choke her damn tongue out of her mouth. Mama Sarah said Aunt Bell never should have taken that man from his wife, when they had a houseful of children to care for.

I guess Aunt Kate was the strongest one. Mama Sarah had a lot of faith and trust in Aunt Kate. Aunt Kate was born October 14, 1925. Mama Sarah's first *"Roaring Twenties"* baby; born the same year of Malcolm X. The same year Nellie Ross took office in the state of Wyoming as the first female Governor elected in the United States. Mama Sarah believed this meant that Aunt Kate was strong and born to be a winner.

My mother, Amy Mae, was the baby and everybody treated her like one. I guess that's why she was so spoiled. Mama Sarah said she always knew when my mother was pregnant with another child. She said she would sleep all the time with her thumb stuck in her mouth.

All of Mama Sarah's children were beautiful children; having smooth brown skin and silky black hair. People said Mama Sarah's grandmamma was a full-blooded Cherokee Indian married to a Black man.

Mama Sarah was a tall robust woman, standing about five seven and weighing almost 200 pounds. Her voice was heavy and loud, and when she sang, it sounded like a roar of thunder from the heart of an angel. She knew everything about everything. There was nothing she hadn't seen or done, and no place she hadn't been, even if it was only in her dreams. Mama Sarah was my Hero!

So, in our house, on that night, December 2, 1950, I was born. Mama Sarah said I was looking around as if I had been here before. She said when she showed me to everyone in the house that night all you could hear were expressions of disgust and regret, which agitated the hell out of Mama Sarah.

"All shoot. Damn Mama Sarah!" One man said. *"She's going to be Black!"*

The tips of my little fingers and my little ears said it all. Yep, I was just as dark skinned as I could be. I guess that's why Mama Sarah always said, *"Black folk have been taught to hate themselves from the cradle to the grave."* This beautiful, healthy baby girl deemed inferior by her own people due to the color of her beautiful dark brown skin. But if the truth be told, this whole concept of hatred for dark skinned people was developed to control the masses and many Black people still buy into this repugnant idea to this very day. Many people settle and accept their dark skin tone, but if they could change it, they would. Why? Because there's an unwritten Law, mentally taught, that Black is not beautiful. That Black is evil, wicked, disgraceful, and everything that's bad. And who wants to be that; no one. But if all people would read and study like Mama Sarah does, no one would have a problem with dark skin at all. Mama Sarah tried to teach them a little knowledge that night. She would give anything to change the mind-set of people in America and around the world.

"Y'all are so stupid!" Mama Sarah yelled at them. *"This baby has inherited the most dominant gene in the whole Universe. The most powerful gene in genetics: Melanin (Carbon)! The most valuable chemical in life! It's omnipresent in nature and it's found everywhere: In the soil; in the oceans, in clouds and even in the stars. It's the closest thing to GOD that anything can get. Remember the words in the Book of our GREAT FATHER, "My People are DESTROYED from the Lack of Knowledge!" Open up a book and read something sometimes; learn about yourself!"* Mama Sarah was furious. She always wanted Black people to embrace the richness of the color of their beautiful skin.

"Oh well, I don't care how much Mama Sarah taught us, we would always forget to remember. But that's okay. I'm glad I was born into this family. I believe I could feel the love and warmth the moment I got here. I wouldn't change a thing. Thank you God for a loving family! No, I wouldn't change a thing."

****

On that same night, December 2, 1950, about three miles away, in an upscale area where the affluent White folks lived, a White family was experiencing a devastating crisis; too shocking to ever speak of again, and leading to the destruction of a loving family forever. Screams were coming from the house so loud that it sounded like a murder was being committed.

"William, please. Please William." A White woman begged her husband. *"She's your child William, can't you see she's bleeding! I beg you William; for the love of God, please stop!"*

A thin, pale, terrified White woman pleaded with her husband to stop, as he literally, unmercifully, beat their sixteen year old daughter into a hemorrhage. He was trying to get information from his daughter that she wouldn't tell him. He responded to his wife in raging anger:

"She's going to tell me who this Nigger is or I'll kill her with my bare hands! Tell me, you whoring bitch! Who touched you? Tell me!"

This gentleman was Williams Kent; a high powered Prosecuting Attorney in Memphis with a reputation of being a notorious gangster Lawyer who enjoyed putting Black men behind bars. The word was he hated Black people, although he employed Black people to cook his food and clean his house. Plus, he also kept a Black mistress for years and fathered two of her children. And now, his daughter, Chrissie, was pregnant, and says the father is a Colored boy.

Blood was everywhere. The more her father beat her, the more Chrissie refused to tell him the boy's name. She would only say:

"I can't tell you Dad. I'm afraid for him!"

Chrissie never told her parents she was pregnant. She was too afraid to tell them. But during her seventh month her parents could see she was pregnant. And that evening, at their dinner table, December 2, 1950, they asked the question and Chrissie admitted she was pregnant and the father was a Colored boy.

Chrissie's screams were so loud until one of the neighbors called the police. When the police arrived and were informed of the circumstances, they pleaded with Attorney Kent to let them call for an ambulance. When the ambulance arrived, Chrissie had fainted, but she was still alive. The medical staff at the hospital was standing by, waiting for her arrival.

Upon her arrival, she was immediately taken to surgery. The surgery went well, but Chrissie was too weak to endure the blows and bruises inflicted upon her by her father. Chrissie died. Her death certificate stated her cause of death was due to complications during childbirth. There was no funeral, only a burial. And a couple of weeks later, the Kent family moved away, leaving the baby at the hospital, and were never heard of again.

The young Black boy, who everyone believed fathered Chrissie's child, suddenly disappeared from the neighborhood too. No one ever heard of him again either. Nonetheless, as the rainbow appears after the rain, a sense of beauty came from this horrible event; a beautiful, tiny baby girl, weighing three pounds and fifteen ounces. You could tell her daddy was a Black man. She looked like a soft, fresh peach, picked from a tree in the Garden of Eden. She had straight silky brown hair, little round eyes and tiny little hands, trying to hold on right from the beginning. Being premature, she had to stay in the hospital a couple of months for special care. Upon her discharge, she was to become a ward of the State.

However, one of the nurses at the hospital became very attached to the little girl and grew to love her very much. The nurse was Valerie Johns, the wife of Deacon Buford Johns, one of the fine deacons at a very popular neighborhood Baptist Church. They were neighbors down the street from Kate and Mama Sarah's home. Mama Sarah did ironing and cooking for them. Nurse Johns wanted to adopt the little girl and take her home. She pleaded with her husband to let her bring this adorable child into their home.

"Buford, can I please bring her home?" Valerie asked her husband. *"I know the hospital will go along with it. She is so quiet and loveable, and she needs special care. And you know no one will care for her like I will. Please Buford, let me bring her home."*

Deacon Johns was a horrible man. He was cruel and pitiless, with a lack of compassion for anyone and didn't care who knew it. He would kick a dying dog if he thought no one would see it. He hated dark-skinned Black people. He only used them for degrading tasks like shinning his shoes and taking out his trash.

He held out to be a devout Christian, holding the high office of Head Deacon in his church. Yet, he had a hand in every underhanded, cunning affair in the Black community. He was the School Master at one of the local Black high schools and was highly respected by many powerful White men in Tennessee. To put it mildly, he was a back stabbing sell-out to every Black person he shook hands with.

Nurse Johns was just the opposite, totally different in every way. A loving, kind woman, who spent most of her time caring for the sick at work and caring for the sick away from work. A true saint the woman was; a true saint.

"Hell naw." Deacon Johns screamed at his wife. *"And that's what I mean. I don't want to hear no damn baby crying all night and then go to work and listen to a bunch of crying Niggers all day. Let one of them White heifers take her home*

with them. It was one of them who laid up and got her. Let one of them take her home."

"Now Buford, let's be real Darling." Valerie said to her husband, as she put her arms around his neck, slightly touching her body to his, rubbing him softly. A gesture she knew would always bring a yes. *"It would be a disgrace for a White nurse to take her home. It wouldn't be fair to their family. Please Darling; she needs a special family like ours to love and care for her."* Valerie kissed her husband softly on his neck as she rubbed him below the torso; knowing in her heart, he was a fool for sex.

"Oh, well." Deacon Johns said. *"I guess it's okay. But the first night she keeps me up all night hollering, it's going be your behind, you understand that?"*

Nurse Johns was so happy. She immediately talked with her superiors at the hospital concerning the adoption. They all thought it was a splendid idea. The hospital immediately started Court proceedings and by the time the baby weighed five pounds, she was ready to go home with Nurse Johns. The hospital staff had a small celebration and toasted to the beautiful baby girl. Nurse Johns named her Virginia Elizabeth Johns and called her Jenny.

****

Three weeks before Ann and Jenny were born Polly Mae Love had a baby too. Polly Mae had moved to the neighborhood in mid-summer, 1948. No one knew where she came from and her kinfolk never visited her. It was as if she was running away from something or someone and never wanted to look back. She attached herself to Mama Sarah and grew very close to her.

Polly Mae rented a house in a shanty little area about a block from Mama Sarah's house. A little area called The Back Alley. The Back Alley was where the poorest of the poor people lived. Polly Mae worked as a maid, like many other women in the neighborhood, to take care of herself.

Mama Sarah could see that Polly Mae was a troubled child, so she took her under her wing as one of her own. Polly Mae was very loving and kind to everyone. Most of the women in the neighborhood were jealous of her though. Mama Sarah said she was every poor man's dream and every poor woman's nightmare.

Polly Mae was what Black folk called paper sack tan. She was five feet two inches, weighing about 110 pounds, with perfect body measurements in all the right places: 32, 21, 36, and being young and very immature, Polly Mae accommodated every man who made his way to her bed. A young, beautiful girl, out on her own, believing every lie a man with a stiff would tell her. Nevertheless, Mama Sarah never looked down on Polly Mae. Mama Sarah looked down on the no good men taking advantage of a deprived child longing to be loved.

When Mama Sarah cooked, she always cooked enough to share with Polly Mae. Mama Sarah helped her organize her little home and taught her to keep her house and her body clean.

Several months later, Polly Mae was pregnant. All those men scratching at her door disappeared.

On November 12, 1950, Polly Mae sent her next door neighbor to tell Mama Sarah she was hurting. Mama Sarah and two of Mama Sarah's friends hurried to Polly Mae's side. Mama Sarah delivered Polly Mae's baby and there was no man anywhere to be found.

Polly Mae's labor was long and hard. She rolled in agony all night long. The result was a ten pound beautiful baby girl, bald-headed, but charming; fat, healthy and whaling as if she was singing a song.

"Oh thank you Mama Sarah." Polly Mae told Mama Sarah. *"I don't know what I would do without you. Bless you Mama Sarah; bless you."*

"Thank you baby;" Mama Sarah said. *"But don't forget to thank God. It was Him who carried you through this ordeal. You are a child of God just as I am. It's Him who looks after you and provides for you, not me. God loves you, you see, He has blessed you with a beautiful, healthy baby girl."* Mama Sarah put the baby in Polly Mae's arms.

"Oh Lord." Mama Sarah said. *"Look at her. She's ready to nurse, too. Come on y'all,"* Mama Sarah said to her friends. *"Let's wash Polly Mae up so the baby can nurse. Don't put too much water on Polly Mae. I don't want her to get sick from all this air coming through these cracks in this house. And Polly Mae, don't let these men come in here trying to nurse you. This milk is for this baby, not them. And don't let anybody mess with you either. You hear me?"*

"Yes, ma'am," Polly Mae answered.

"When we finish cleaning y'all up," Mama Sarah said. *"I'm going home and get some fruit for you to eat. When I come back, I'll clean up the rest of this mess. We're not going to leave y'all by yourself. One of us will be right here with you until you're on your feet again. My Lord, baby."* Mama Sarah said. *"You're going to catch hell trying to make Black folk think this is a Black man's baby. I know every man around here is on his knees praying right now. But I'm here to tell 'em, you can get up brother, you ain't got nothing to worry about."* Mama Sarah and her two friends laughed.

16

"Polly Mae, you sure this is a Black man's baby?" Mama Sarah said to her.

"Yes ma'am," Polly Mae said, smiling. *"Robert Lowell is her daddy."*

"Robert Lowell!" Mama Sarah bucked her eyes in disbelief. *"Well, if he is, you sure have fooled the hell out of me."* Mama Sarah and her friends all laughed again. Polly Mae laughed too.

Mama Sarah believed a White man had fathered Polly Mae's baby and Polly Mae was afraid to say anything about it. White men have been making their way to the Black woman's bed for centuries and nothing has been done about it. Mama Sarah believed that the White man has a deep, powerful connection to the Black woman that he himself doesn't understand. Mama Sarah said, whatever it is, it will someday reveal itself. Truth crushed to the ground will rise again.

"What you gonna name her?" Mama Sarah asked Polly Mae.

"I've got her name all picked out." Polly Mae said. *"I want to name her after you, Mama Sarah, because you are so dear to me. And I want to name her after me because I want her to know how dear she is to me. So I put our names together to call her Pottianna; Pottianna Love. And we're gonna call her Pot, because she's my pot of gold at the end of my rainbow."* Polly Mae had a glowing smile on her face.

"That's sweet child; that's really sweet." Mama Sarah told her. *"God's going to bless y'all too; and this little girl is going to make you proud."* Everyone smiled as love filled the room.

Ann, Pot and Jenny, another chapter in the lives of Black folk. Who knows what they'll become. Well, in the words of Mama Sarah, *"It's not our concern. It's between them and God. Our job is to love them as God and Jesus loves us. We must teach them to love, believe in the words and works of Jesus, and live Holy; to manifest the promises of God in their lives. And as all magnificent human beings, they'll take their place on this beautiful earth, live their beautiful lives, and be just fine. Yes, they will all be just fine!"*

Chapter 2

Children always remember

Mama Sarah said I grew like wildfire. She said one day I was walking and before she knew it, I was bending down trying to tie my shoes. Mama Sarah said I came here talking. She said I first started talking with my eyes. She said my eyes could tell her everything about me; when I was sleepy, when I was hurting, hiding something, and even when I had peed my pants. So when I wanted a big laugh out of her, I would stand in front of her, fold my little arms together, wearing a pair of shades to hide my eyes. Mama Sarah would laugh so loud, grab me, and give me a great big hug, squeezing me real tight. I was a great joy to Mama Sarah as a child. She loves me very much.

I found those shades in the park one evening. Mama Sarah said I could keep them because there was no way to determine who they belonged to. They were much too big for my eyes, but she said I would grow to them. So I took them home and put them in my shoebox. Everybody in our house had a shoebox. The shoebox was where we put our very personal things: toothbrush, toothpaste, perfume; anything personal we didn't want anyone to mess with. It was a strict rule in our house; you never go in anybody's shoebox without their permission.

When Mama Sarah was sad or something was troubling her, I would go to my shoebox and put those shades on. Somehow, this little gesture would ease the tension and make Mama Sarah smile. Laughter was a very good medicine for making a bad situation a bit more acceptable.

Mama Sarah said I was into everything as a baby. Crawling, pulling things down, she said she had to spank my hands almost every day. She said I was playing patty-cake very early; identifying my eyes, ears, nose, and mouth at six months old and I walked at nine months. Mama Sarah kept several little switches on top of the refrigerator just for me. Amy Mae was so lazy. She had no time for me at all. Mama Sarah said all her time and energy went into trying to get my daddy back.

****

In the fall of 1953, Charlie Murphy finally showed back up in Memphis. He was driving a new car, bragging and boasting to the neighbors about how much money he was making at an automobile plant in Michigan. He went about telling everybody he had come back to get Amy Mae and his children. He was going to take them back to Detroit with him.

When the word got back to Mama Sarah, she turned pea green with anger. The family had to hold her down to keep her from getting her gun, going to find him.

The news about Charlie Murphy's intentions was the talk of the neighborhood and Mama Sarah didn't like it, not one bit. As the subject was talked about at their house, Mama Sarah blurted out in anger:

"If Charlie Murphy brings his ass to this house talking about taking my children, I will kill his ass. Amy Mae, you wrote him almost every day and he has not written you, not one time. He has not sent any money or food, or anything to help with his

20

children. As far as I'm concerned, he doesn't have any children at this residence at all."

Amy Mae didn't say a word. She just sat there, on the couch, with tears rolling down her face. Mama Sarah walked over to Amy Mae, shouting at her.

"What in the hell are you crying for Amy Mae?" Mama Sarah shouted. *"You should be glad I'm standing up for you!"*

Mama Sarah knew in her heart that Amy Mae still wanted Charlie Murphy. It was hard for her to accept the fact that Amy Mae was so vulnerable. How could Amy Mae want a man who had fathered three children with her and had never given her a dime to take care of them? Mama Sarah shouted at her again:

"This man has come back to Memphis and hasn't even come by to see you or his children, and he has the gall to canvas the neighborhood spreading lies, telling people what he's here to do. What in the hell are you crying for? Talk to me, Amy Mae!" Mama Sarah was furious.

Amy Mae burst into tears, weeping, as she tried to talk.

"I don't know! I don't know, Mama!" Amy Mae said. *"All I know is that I love him! I just love him!"*

Mama Sarah stood there with hurt in her eyes, holding herself back from grabbing Amy Mae and beating some sense into her

head. **Mama Sarah was dumbfounded. She couldn't' say a word. Amy Mae continued, as she wept.**

"You've never liked Charlie, Mama. He would have married me after Mark was born, but you wouldn't let him. You know how he loves Benjamin. He really loves all of us, but you never wanted him around. That's why he hasn't come by here yet, Mama! He can feel you don't want him here! You've got to give him a chance to show you what he's made of!"

Mama Sarah shouted out in a rage:

"Give him a chance to show me what he's made of? How many chances does a man need Amy Mae? This man has been in your life for over six years. Over six years! What has he shown anybody? Three children, that's all! I've helped you raise these boys, not him! Now I'm helping you raise his daughter! How many chances does a man need? It's not me Amy Mae! Don't put this mess on me! I'm here to help you! What in the hell has he done?"

Tears poured from Amy Mae's eyes like rain and her feelings were very hurt. Everyone stood there in silence. Hurt and pain was felt by everyone. Kate intervened to calm the unhappy occurrence. Kate held Mama Sarah by the arm as she rubbed Mama Sarah's back; speaking to her softly.

"Mama, come on now." Kate commented. "Amy Mae is grown. We have to understand that she can make her own decisions. We've got to let her go. We can't keep treating her like a child. She'll be all right. Trust me Mama. Amy Mae will be all right."

22

Mama Sarah started to cry. Trembling in her voice, as she talked:

> *"I don't want my child to make a fool of her self; and I don't care what nobody says, she's not taking this baby nowhere. It's cold up North and y'all know Amy Mae is not going to take care of this baby."*

Mama Sarah became overwhelmed with emotions. Kate held her close, rocking her gently until she calmed down. Polly Mae was there and managed to quiet down Amy Mae and comfort her.

A few days later, Charlie Murphy conjured up enough nerves to face Mama Sarah. People laughed about how he walked up to Mama Sarah, took his hat off and bowed, as an ultimate gesture of respect for a gracious lady. His hat was shaking in his hand as he tried to convey to Mama Sarah that his intentions were straight from the heart.

> *"Ms. Sarah,"* Charlie Murphy stated. *"I know you don't think much of me as a man, but I'm a hard worker, and I love Amy Mae. I don't care how many women I've had; don't none of them touch Amy Mae. Amy Mae stays on my mind more than any woman I know. And I know these boys and this baby girl are mine. They look just like me. I know I'm their daddy, and I'm going to take care of 'em too. And I came here today to ask you if Amy Mae can go back with me to Detroit. I promise you I'll take good care of her."*

Before Mama Sarah could give him a straight answer, Amy Mae was packed and ready to go. She took Mark and Ben and left Ann with Mama Sarah. Mama Sarah and Ann were each other's world. She made Ann just as happy as Ann made her. They were a match made by God.

****

I didn't see my mother, father, and brothers again until I was five years old. My next three years were filled with all kinds of events I love to talk about and remember.

Our family was getting smaller and smaller. Everybody was leaving the nest. Cousin Sugar got married and moved to Atlanta, taking with her, Jerry and Terry, her two eight-year old ruthless twins. They were monsters from hell. Drinking up all the milk, eating all the bread and they acted like they were still hungry. I was so glad to see them go. I hugged and kissed them goodbye.

The only ones left at home were me, Mama Sarah, Aunt Kate, Cousin Mable Lee, and her three boys. I couldn't wait for some man to come along and take Mable Lee and the boys with him. Her boys never let me watch my favorite TV programs and they would hit me with chinaberries from our chinaberry tree. When I would go to sleep, they would put chewing gum in my hair so I would cry when I got my hair combed. They also made faces at me when Mama Sarah turned her back. But in spite of all that, I was still a happy child.

Finally, Cousin Mable Lee got a job at the county hospital and she and her boys moved to their own place. I was so happy to see them go. Now Pot and I had the whole back yard all to ourselves. We made a playhouse under the big tree in the back yard and baked mud pies every day. Mama Sarah taught us how to make sea grass dolls and how to braid their hair. Ms. Polly Mae gave us her old dresses to play dress-up in. Pot and I got along very well. We were like sisters. We could play together everyday, all day long, without any quarreling at all.

Sometimes I played with Jenny, too. Mama Sarah took in ironing for Deacon Johns and cooked for them when Ms. Linda was ill with one of her migraine headaches. Ms. Linda Jernigan was Deacon Johns' live in assistant. Mama Sarah said those headaches were really hangovers Ms. Linda had after boozing half of the night, trying to silence her conscience from whipping her after she helped Deacon Johns put Nurse Johns in an insane asylum.

I know that sounds crazy, but I would hear Mama Sarah and her best friend, Ms. Mozella, talking about it when Mama Sarah was combing my hair. I guess they thought I was too little to understand what they were talking about and never gave their conversations a second thought, but I would listen to everything they said. I learned a lot and I knew all kind of stuff about grown folk business.

Mama Sarah said Ms. Linda worked at the school where Deacon Johns worked. He was a schoolmaster at one of the most prestigious Black High Schools in this city. He was well known by all the important people in Memphis, Black and White. Mama Sarah said he was the biggest fake in town, a superficial fraud. She said everybody knew Ms. Linda was his woman. He took her with him every time he went out of town and they spent late nights together, working at his office.

Nurse Johns knew about this affair too, but she kept quiet about it. She loved Deacon Johns and wanted to save her marriage. Being a loving, devoted wife, and giving him all the sex any man would ever need, wasn't enough to satisfy his scandalous nature. Nonetheless, she never quarreled with him nor did she question his arrogant behavior, or his whereabouts. She deliberately disregarded all evidence of his deception and carried on as a happy, content wife. She didn't want to disclose the shame and dishonor manifesting in her household, especially to her co-workers and her church.

Deacon Johns felt just the opposite. He wanted Nurse Johns to know about his affairs. He wanted her to be so jealous, depressed and sad until she would literally go mad.

One night, things didn't go as they usually did. Deacon Johns had been gone for three days, attending a conference in Knoxville, Tennessee. Nurse Johns had had it with his lies and him being away from home so many nights. She was a meek and gentle person, very slow to anger, and always hiding her feelings inside. But this night, things didn't go as they usually did. It was about nine o'clock p.m. Mama Sarah had just finished giving Jenny her bath and putting her to bed.

A few minutes later, Deacon Johns came home. He had been drinking heavy that night because he was acting a fool. He came in the house, rushing through the door, calling Nurse Johns loud, as if he wanted to fight.

"Val, where in the hell are you?" He shouted.

Nurse Johns didn't answer him. She just looked at him with hate in her eyes and kept rolling her hair. Deacon Johns rushed over to her, pulled her from her chair, and pushed her toward the kitchen.

"Get your ass in that kitchen!" He shouted. *"And fix me something to eat!"*

Nurse Johns still didn't say a word. She put her rollers down and went into the kitchen to warm him something to eat. Mama Sarah intervened, hoping to soften the exclamation of anger in the air.

"Can I get your dinner for you Deacon?" Mama Sarah asked. *"Nurse Johns has to work in the morning; I can get your food for you."*

"Hell naw!" Deacon Johns shouted. *"I want my wife to fix my food. That's her job. That's what I married her ass for. She's mine! And Ms. Sarah this is married folk business. As far as I'm concerned you're done here for the night. You can go home!"*

Nurse Johns was highly offended by Deacon Johns' insulting remarks to Mama Sarah but she still didn't say a word. She just stood there, at the stove, fixing his plate. There was a long sharp butcher knife on the counter near her. Deacon Johns walked up behind Nurse Johns and started rubbing her butt and putting his hand between her legs as if he wanted to make love to her right there, in the kitchen, at that very moment. Nurse Johns disregarded his sexual advances and harshly pushed him away. Deacon Johns shouted at her like a crazy man.

"What the hell's wrong with you, got dammit!" He shouted.

But before he could say another word, Nurse Johns whirled around and whacked him across the chin with that butcher knife. Deacon Johns squalled like a polecat and blood splashed everywhere. Mama Sarah was flabbergasted she didn't know Nurse Johns had it in her.

Everything was chaotic for a moment, as Deacon Johns and Nurse Johns scuffled over the knife. Somehow, Deacon Johns forced the knife from Nurse Johns' hand and stumbled to the telephone and called the police. The police arrived within minutes. And all you could hear was Deacon Johns shouting:

"This woman tried to kill me!" "This woman tried to kill me!"

The police called for an ambulance to take Deacon Johns to the hospital and they took Nurse Johns to jail. Mama Sarah locked their house up and took Jenny home with her.

The news rapidly spread throughout the neighborhood and all you could hear for the next few days was Nurse Johns tried to kill Deacon Johns.

And sometimes, as things happen, Deacon Johns got his wish. Nurse Johns had a mental break down after being locked up, and was taken to a local hospital for observation. Deacon Johns managed to convince the doctors at that hospital that Nurse Johns was a threat to him, little Jenny, and to herself. The doctors agreed with Deacon Johns, they had Nurse Johns admitted and she stayed in an insane asylum for many years.

A couple of months after Nurse Johns was admitted to the asylum, Deacon Johns moved Ms. Linda into his home to help care for Jenny. The rest is history. Ms. Linda was there to stay. She soon became a part of the family and fit right in with everyone else.

After Nurse Johns was admitted to an insane asylum, Pot, Jenny and I were like peas in a pod. We played together mostly every day. We even helped Mama Sarah work in the backyard garden. She taught us how to plant seeds and blackberries grew all along the back yard fence. Mama Sarah taught us Bible verses and how to pray our prayers. She loved the earth. When she worked in the garden, she would rub the soil on her arms and hands, thanking God for Mother Earth. Mama Sarah would pray out loud, saying:

"God said, Behold, I have given you every herb bearing seed, which is upon the face of all the Earth. I have given you every tree, which is the fruit of a tree yielding seed. To you it shall be for meat. Be fruitful and multiply, replenish the Earth and subdue it. God bless Mother Earth."

Pot, Jenny, and I would laugh and snicker. We thought Mama Sarah was crazy. We would sometimes pretend to be her when we played in our playhouse. We loved her though, and we learned so much from her. She taught us that nothing is greater than God. She said we are Gods and we must think like God. She taught us that nothing is more valuable than a true friend; that the more you give, the more you will receive, and lots of other good things. To this day, every year, I plant something in the Earth just to see life grow. Mama Sarah was a whole package of love, and she gave plenty of love to us.

****

Friday, December 2, 1955, was my birthday. I was going to be five years old. I dreaded that birthday. That was the year I was supposed to go live with Amy Mae and Charlie Murphy. I didn't want to live with them. I wanted to stay with Mama Sarah. I also couldn't leave Pot and Jenny. I believed I would wither away and die being away from them. I wanted to see my brothers, but I couldn't leave Pot and Jenny.

At this same time, Amy Mae and Charlie Murphy announced they were getting married, and had put me in their wedding as their flower girl. I told Mama Sarah I didn't want to do it, but she said I was going to do it or she was going to whip my butt. She said they wanted to keep me in Detroit and send me to school with my brothers. I told her I was going to run away and never come back. That did it. Mama Sara jerked me up, threw me across her lap, and tore my behind up.

Yes, finally, Charlie Murphy asked Amy Mae for her hand in marriage and she said "yes." They set the date for May 12, 1956, and were busy making wedding plans. Kate was very excited and eager to help. Kate liked Charlie Murphy and believed he would make a good husband for Amy Mae. Mama Sarah was happy too, although she pretended she wasn't. She was really missing her baby girl and didn't want any man to have her, regardless of who he was.

Everyone went to Detroit to the wedding. Mama Sarah packed all of Ann's clothes and they caught the train to Detroit. This was a sad occasion for Mama Sarah. All she could think about was leaving Ann in Detroit with her parents. Parting from Ann was hard for Mama Sarah and every bit of it showed on her face.

Amy Mae and Charlie Murphy felt that sending Ann to school up North with her brothers would give her a better education. Ann was their child and Mama Sarah felt she didn't have the right to tell them they couldn't keep her.

The wedding was nice. Kate had gone to Detroit two weeks earlier to help get everything together. Amy Mae was a beautiful bride. All the colorful decorations were beautiful and Ann made the perfect little flower girl. The food at the reception was a mega feast and the spirits flowed for every glass all night long. Leave everything to Kate and everyone was guaranteed to have a great time. All of the family was there, some meeting Ann for the very first time.

My momma and daddy were finally married. I can't remember if I was happy for them or not. I guess I was really just a child and didn't realize how important marriage is at that time. All I could think about was Mama Sarah leaving me in Detroit. I guess the thought of her leaving me there made me a nervous wreck.

A couple of days after the wedding, Mama Sarah was preparing to ride back to Memphis with Aunt Kate and Big Daddy. When she put her suitcase in Big Daddy's car, I started to scream and cry. I grabbed Mama Sarah's leg and held on for dear life. Nothing and no one could shut me up. I cried myself into a fever. I cried, and I barfed. I cried and I barfed. I believed my daddy thought I didn't want to live with him, but it wasn't that at all. I wanted to live with Mama Sarah so I could be with Pot and Jenny.

Finally, Aunt Kate asked Mama Sarah to take me back with her so I wouldn't make myself sick. I think Amy Mae was just as happy as I was. I was so glad to be in that car on my way back to Memphis; I could have shouted Glory, Hallelujah!

I slept most of the way back, and in no time we were crossing the Memphis and Arkansas Bridge. I was so happy. I was going to go to school with Pot and Jenny after all.

The next day, Jenny and Pot were very happy to see me. I had no idea they would miss me so much. I was so happy for us to be together again. That same night, Mama Sarah had to serve a party for Deacon Johns. He was having businessmen from Nashville and Knoxville meeting at his home. Some of them were White men. Mama Sarah had to work that whole day at his home, making sure everything was just right. Deacon Johns always wanted his guests to be impressed, so he paid Mama Sarah well for her excellent service.

All that day, Pot and I played with Jenny in her backyard while Mama Sarah cooked. Ms. Polly Mae had to work so Pot stayed with us. Jenny had everything in her backyard. A sand box, a swing, and a playhouse made of real wood. I laughed so much that day; everything tickled me. Mama Sarah had to call to me a number of times, telling me to stop laughing so loud. I was so happy to be at home again.

That evening, Mama Sarah gave me, Pot and Jenny a bath in the tin tub on Deacon Johns' back porch. She put us in our nightclothes and I was praying that Pot and I would spend the night.

During Deacon Johns' dinner parties, Mama Sarah would bring us all kinds of good things to eat: sausage balls, shrimp, little pieces of steak wrapped in bacon, finger sandwiches, dip, and homemade Hawaiian punch.

I got my wish that night, Pot and I did spend the night. All three of us, Pot, Jenny and I, were up half the night. We watched the late show on television and Pot and I got a chance to sleep at the foot of Jenny's big soft bed.

Deacon Johns' dinner party was good too. We could hear nice music and laughter all night long. Mama Sarah was very tired the next day. Aunt Kate encouraged her to stay in bed and I rubbed her back, her arms, and her legs with some strong warm hyssop tea.

The months went by fast and we stayed at Jenny's house just as much as we stayed at home. Deacon Johns had important people down from Nashville almost every weekend. Mama Sarah told Ms. Mozella they were meeting to talk about the integration of public schools in Memphis. Mama Sarah and Ms. Mozella weren't happy about it though. They said our little Black children were being put in a very precarious situation. I didn't care what kind of situation we were put in, I was ready to go to school with Pot and Jenny. I was ready to be the best student I could be.

At registration, Mama Sarah made sure we were all in the same class. She waited for Deacon Johns to register Jenny and she would register me and Pot in that same class. Mama Sarah believed Deacon Johns knew the best teachers for Jenny to get the best education and Mama Sarah was determined to make sure Pot and I got the best education too.

Chapter 3

The joy and pain of childhood

I was very happy with school, that is, most of the time. But, as I reminisce about some of the things that happened to us in fourth grade, I cringe. Bell Bellevue, a girl in our class, was a horrible person. She hated Jenny with a passion. I couldn't understand her feelings, because Jenny was nice to everybody. Jenny would bring treats to school for all the children in our class. When Ms. Linda would buy cookies and candy for Jenny, Jenny would slip and bring whole bags to school in her book bag to share with all of us. Although Jenny shared with Bell Bellevue, Bell Bellevue would still throw mud on Jenny's pretty dresses during recess. All three of us, Jenny, Pot and I were afraid of Bell Bellevue. So, Pot and I would go to the bathroom with Jenny, take wet paper towels and wash the mud from Jenny's dresses as best as we could. We were afraid to tell our teachers, and heaven help us if we had told our parents. This abuse went on for months, and we would just suck it up, and act like nothing had happened. I guess that wasn't good enough for Bell Bellevue.

After months of seeing Jenny wear beautiful dresses and fancy ribbons in her hair; and seeing Deacon Johns pick Jenny up in his shiny new car, Bell Bellevue couldn't stand it anymore. I guess her bullying, and terrorizing us just wasn't enough. And on this particular day, early that morning, I heard her tell Jenny in the cloakroom:

"I'm going to get you at recess!"

My heart almost stopped beating, and that sudden feeling of fear that came upon me caused a big lump to form in my throat, almost bringing tears to my eyes. I thought to myself, *"Oh God, why did I have to be in here to hear that?"*

Jenny looked at me and I looked at Jenny; we were both afraid. Jenny's skin color usually changed to pink or red when she was afraid, but this time Jenny's skin color changed to white. I believe Bell Bellevue scared Jenny so, it made her blood disappear.

All of a sudden, Ms. Daniels, our teacher, called to us.

"Virginia and Sarah come out of the cloakroom and take your seats. You've had enough time to hang your coats."

Jenny and I walked slowly out of the cloakroom. Pot was shocked to see that powerless look of fear on our face. Ms. Daniels was very adamant about her rule of absolutely no talking, so we couldn't say a word. The morning went by slowly and the lunch bell rang. This could have been Jenny's last meal, but she couldn't eat a thing. That big lump in my throat, coupled with my peanut butter sandwich, made it hard for me to swallow, so I couldn't eat either. Pot was on detention, that day, for being late for school so she had to eat lunch and spend her recess time in the classroom.

Bell Bellevue hated Jenny so much until she was standing on the playground waiting for us to come outside. All the children at school had to go outside for recess. The cafeteria monitors wouldn't let any students stay inside. Jenny and I stayed inside until they insisted that we go to the playground.

Bell Bellevue was twice our size. She was a rough looking girl with freckles across her nose. Her sandy hair was of a coarse thick texture and her plaits were always braided upside down. Her arms and legs were very muscular, and that humiliating frown she wore on her face was that of a jackal about to corner its game.

The minute Jenny and I stepped on the playground, Bell Bellevue grabbed both of us. I broke away and started to run, hoping Jenny was running beside me. I didn't care if the children laughed at me; I wanted to save my life.

Suddenly, I looked back and Jenny wasn't there. All the children were gathered around Jenny and Bell Bellevue. I couldn't see either of them. I was very afraid, but I had to go back. I couldn't leave Jenny by herself. I went back and made my way through the crowd. Bell Bellevue was tearing Jenny apart. I truly believe she was actually trying to kill Jenny.

Jenny's face was bruised and red. Dirt was all over Jenny's clothes and in her hair. Bell Bellevue was on top of Jenny with those huge barbaric hands around Jenny's neck. Bell Bellevue's thumbs were positioned, squeezing Jenny's throat. Jenny was laying limp with her eyes closed. I thought Jenny was dead. I panicked! I let out a loud scream, and started to fight Bell Bellevue with all I had! Still, she wouldn't let go of Jenny's throat.

All of a sudden, Pot came from out of nowhere, holding a brick in her hand. Pot hit Bell Bellevue in the head with that brick and blood splattered everywhere. Bell Bellevue fell to the ground like a wounded wild buffalo. The children started to run and scream, scattering all over the playground. The teachers heard the noise and came running. Thank God that both Jenny and Bell Bellevue lived and can tell this same story today.

This incident was very painful for Deacon Johns. And believe me, some heads rolled for this terrible act of violence. Deacon Johns loved Jenny and the whole faculty at our school was held accountable. The school system paid dearly for Jenny's injuries and the principal along with several teachers were replaced. Deacon Johns transferred Jenny to Mother Mary's Catholic School for Girls. Jenny completed Elementary school and Junior High school at Mother Mary's.

As for me and Pot, the whole ordeal was devastating. Elementary and Junior High school were not the same without Jenny. One thing for sure, Bell Bellevue never bothered us again. Pot and I saw her at school every day, but she kept her distance. At times I felt sorry for Bell Bellevue. She looked so sad and hurt. Sometimes I prayed that God would uplift her downtrodden Spirit and bring her happiness again.

Life drastically changed for me and Pot. We had to walk to school every day. I couldn't believe how cold it was. The wind was like ice blowing against my face. Mama Sarah wrapped my scarf around my face and put two pairs of gloves on my hands, but I was still cold. I missed riding to school with Jenny in Deacon Johns' warm car. Pot and I walked along wishing those good old days were here again.

****

Deacon Johns not only transferred Jenny to another school, he did everything he could to keep her away from us for good. The only place we saw each other was at church. Deacon Johns didn't want Jenny with us at church either, but he couldn't show hate in his heart for children at church. Deacon Johns faked his love for us the best he could and we took advantage of the situation, having fun together more than ever during our time at church.

One night during Revival, Pot, Jenny and I were in the church kitchen on the floor playing jacks. All of a sudden, Ms. Pearl, the head usher, appeared.

"What y'all doing back here?" Ms. Pearl asked us. *"Y'all supposed to be in the sanctuary!"*

"We were praying, Sister Pearl," Jenny said.

"Stop lying in the house of the Lord! Ms. Pearl shouted. *I'm telling your mammy and your pappy so they can whip y'all butts. How old are y'all?"* Ms. Pearl asked us?

"We're all nine Sister Pearl." Jenny answered. *"Nine years old,"*

"Come on here." Sister Pearl said. *"All y'all go get on the mourner's bench, so y'all can get saved. Y'all old enough, back here playing and lying in the house of the Lord."*

Sister Pearl marched all three of us to the front of the church and put us on the mourner's bench. We were so embarrassed. I was glad Mama Sarah wasn't at church that night. She would have torn my behind up.

Later that evening, when I got home, I told Mama Sarah Pot, Jenny, and I were going to be baptized. She hugged me and was happy for us. She got on the telephone, called and told everybody we were getting baptized. And to this day she still doesn't know how it happened.

The day came and we all got baptized. Many of our church members shouted and ran all over the church; emotions were very high. I didn't know about Pot or Jenny, but as for me, I didn't feel anything. I was scared and I didn't know what to do. I didn't know if I was a sinner or what. People were shouting and running all around the church. But I felt the same as I did before I was baptized. I prayed in my mind, *"God, please don't let me be a sinner! Please God; let The Holy Ghost come forth!"* But nothing happened.

Later that evening after dinner, Mama Sarah and I were in the kitchen putting away the dishes. Mama Sarah could see something was bothering me, so she asked me what was wrong.

"You all right, child?" Mama Sarah asked.

"Yes ma'am." I replied.

"Now you know I know better than that." Mama Sarah said. *"What's bothering you?"*

"Mama," I said, sighing. *"When I was baptized today, I didn't feel anything different. I was just wet, that's all. The Holy Ghost didn't get in me at all. I'm wondering why The Holy Ghost passed me by."*

"Oh my darling; my darling child," Mama Sarah said to Ann. *"Please don't think that. The Holy Ghost is the Holy Spirit of God and it dwells within everyone. It's our God given goodness, our godly thoughts, our godly power, our divine nature, our true heart, our love, our sound mind, and everything that is very good. Every human being on this earth is Spirit and we're perfect. We just have to use our mind to realize it. God loves you Ann. He knows your true heart and every thought that comes into your precious little mind. Being baptized is simply a sacred symbolic act of admitting a person into Christianity. All that shouting and running around the church are emotional expressions of happiness and joy of becoming a Christian."*

Mama Sarah took Ann by her hand as she said: *"Listen to me Ann. God gave you this gift of life. You came from God and everything that God is you are. Your Sprit is God dwelling within your body and soul. The breath that you breathe is the breath of God. Right now, you are a child, but your understanding will increase with wisdom and knowledge. What we're going to do now is spend more time meditating and studying God's Word. You will then understand and know the power of God within you. And to answer your question Ann, the Holy Ghost didn't pass you by. The Holy Ghost is surely within you. I can see it in your eyes."* Mama Sarah smiled.

Mama Sarah went on and on that day, teaching Ann about the Great "I AM" that dwells within us. Ann was relieved after talking with Mama Sarah. She never second guessed her spirituality ever again. Ann grew in wisdom and knowledge and took God with her all the days of her life. Ann reverenced our Father God, Forever.

****

Pot and I sweated through Elementary school without Jenny and made the best of it. Our most fun classes were Music and PE. I favored any class that helped me shape and tone my developing body. My goal was to be the best majorette my High School ever had. I practiced every day to develop the muscles in my legs so they would stand out and look strong. I knew to be chosen as a new majorette, I had to be the best.

Pot loved singing. She had a beautiful sounding voice. Everybody loved to hear her sing. She always got an A in music. I hated music. Most of the songs we sang were slave songs and songs about the old South. Mama Sarah told me to never sing songs like that. She said it was like telling God you love the idea of being a slave. So I didn't sing, I just moved my mouth, pretending to sing. One afternoon, after music in our classroom, Pot confronted me.

"Ann, you weren't even singing. I believe Ms. Pugh knew it too."

"No she didn't," I said. *But if she did, I don't care. Mama Sarah told me not to sing songs like that. She said it's like telling God we love the idea of being a slave."*

Pot laughed. *"Girl, you know your grandmamma is crazy. Singing ain't got nothing to do with slavery. You better sing those songs or get an F in Music. You know Ms. Pugh isn't going for that."*

"Okay, I'll sing," I said *"but don't tell Mama Sarah I sang songs like that. She'll call this school on the carpet and my butt along with it! You know she believes in freedom and justice with all her heart!"*

"Okay, okay!" Pot said. *"Calm down. You know I'm not going to tell. Your grandmamma is not only crazy; she's a strange woman too. She's the only person I've ever known to put all that junk on the walls in her bathroom. Nobody wants to read that stuff! But every time I use y'all bathroom, I find myself reading it over and over again. I can say most of that stuff from memory: Fourscore and seven years ago."*

"Okay Pot!" I said. *"That's enough about my grandmamma."* Pot laughed.

Pot was right. Mama Sarah had papered the wall in the bathroom with all kinds of important documents, poems, and letters: The Gettysburg Address, The Lord's Prayer, letters written by Dr. King, a letter written by Willie Lynch, frightening newspaper articles and much more. I was almost afraid to be in the bathroom by myself. All those declarations and proclamations appeared to be jumping right out at me. But those letters and documents were very dear to Mama Sarah. She recited lines from them all the time. That's why I knew she wasn't crazy. She was smart. She carried more knowledge around in her head than anybody I've ever known.

I did sing those songs and Pot sang too. We sang and looked stupid. Our teacher sang right along with us. I guess it never occurred to her that the lyrics in those songs were degrading to us and caused hurt and pain to our pride.

"Okay, class." Ms. Pugh said. *"One more time, **SING!**"*

The children sang with robust, very vigorously:

"I wish I was in the land of cotton;
Old times there are not forgotten
Look away look away, look away, Dixie Land
I wish I was in Dixie, Hooray! Hooray!
In Dixie Land I'll take my stand to live and die in Dixie
Away, away, away down south in Dixie
Away, away, away down south in Dixie"

"Okay, class." Ms. Pugh said. *"Put away your music books and take out your math books. Doing your study hour, read*

41

over the lyrics to <u>Oh, Susanna</u> and <u>Old Folks at Home</u>. We'll sing those songs on Monday."

Not only could Pot sing she could dance too. She stayed in the mirror all the time, watching her self dance to music on the radio. When a dance contest was part of our fun, Pot was always the winner. Mama Sarah often told Pot to sit her fast tail down and act like a decent young lady. I think that message went in one of Pot's ears and out her other ear.

Pot never stopped dancing. It was something about her that I couldn't understand. It was as if something was on the inside of her trying to tell you something. You could see it in her eyes. We didn't have any secrets but I felt she was hiding something terrible inside. When she spent the night with us, she would sometimes wake me up crying out in her sleep. I feared something bad had happened to Pot and she was afraid to tell anyone.

Ms. Polly Mae was a very good mother. She loved Pot with all her heart. She tried to give Pot everything. I can't say I liked the way she went about doing it, but I guess it was all she knew how to do. I heard Mama Sarah and Ms. Mozella talking and they said Ms. Polly Mae was running a transient house. They said Ms. Polly Mae was selling after hour liquor for the neighborhood liquor store and the owner of the liquor store was a White man. I dared not to ever mention this to anyone. Mama Sarah would have scolded me to no end.

****

Mama Sarah and Ms. Mozella talked about all kinds of things happening in the Back Alley. Many people in the neighborhood would never be caught back there, and if you lived in the Back Alley, many people wouldn't associate with you. The police were there almost every night harassing and arresting the poor people.

All the drinking and gambling going on back there brought on a police raid almost every weekend. Mama Sarah said she was afraid that someday something bad would go down in the Back Alley and Ms. Polly Mae would find herself right in the middle of it. She said she prayed for Ms. Polly Mae and asked God to keep her safe.

Although the Back Alley was a bad place, Mama Sarah was always going there doctoring the sick and helping pregnant ladies have their babies. She kept Pot at home with us most of the time. We played in the backyard making mud pies and jumping hot peas until we were out of breath. Aunt Kate took us to the library on Tuesdays and Mama Sarah read the Bible to us every Wednesday night. She let us help with canning; a method of putting fruit and vegetables in mason jars to be eaten throughout the winter. We helped her bake cakes at Christmas and make homemade ice cream on the 4th of July. Mama Sarah was so good to us.

Pot and I thought about Jenny every day. We wanted her with us, but we knew that was out of the question as long as Deacon Johns was around. But even as children, we had our ways of getting around the rules of the grownups.

One afternoon, Mama Sarah sent me to take two jars of peach preserves to Ms. Linda. Doing my brief moments there, Jenny passed me a note, which said.

"The next time you go to the store, check for a note in a small bucket under the broken board on the fence in our backyard. There's a note there for you and Pot."

I was so anxious to tell Pot. We went to the store and did as the note directed and there in the bucket was a note from Jenny. This was the best idea Jenny had ever had. It brought so much laughter and happiness to our souls! Anytime Mama Sarah asked me and Pot to go to the store, we were happy to say yes.

Jenny would write us a note and we would write her one back. This went on for months. It was our little secret and no one knew but the three of us. The content of the notes were only kiddish jokes; but, they brought us so much laughter. One of Jenny's notes read:

"Daddy went to sleep yesterday and I rubbed his head with honey. Bees chased him all over the backyard."

Pot and I laughed until our stomachs turned, just thinking of that hilarious sight. Pot once wrote to Jenny, telling her I caught a charley horse in my leg, and when she jerked the charley horse out, I broke wind and blew over two of Mama Sarah's flower pots. We would pass notes and laugh. It was so much fun.

****

Elementary school turned out very good for all three of us. We passed many of our subjects with an A. We were very smart. We could read well and had good study habits. Although everything was going well for me, I never knew when Amy Mae and Charlie Murphy would demand that I come and live with them. They didn't like the South and were not happy with my going to school here. But, I wanted to be with Mama Sarah and I couldn't think of ever leaving Pot and Jenny. I would pray and ask God to keep me, Mama Sarah, Pot, and Jenny together forever.

Finally, elementary school was over and we were getting away from Bell Bellevue. Her family moved and she had to attend school in another district. Pot and I were glad for the good news. We did the chicken dance all over the backyard. We couldn't wait to tell Jenny. Maybe Deacon Johns would let her come back to public school and we would be in the same classes like before. A few weeks later, during our summer break, Pot and I took a few moments for a little girl talk.

"Ann," Pot said. *"Can you believe we are on our way to Junior High School? On our next birthday we'll be thirteen years old. I'm going to wear my skirts so tight I can barely squeeze into 'em. And when all those new boys at our new school see me, they'll want to hold me close and grind on me to a slow love song."*

I laughed at Pot and said: *"And while you're all wrapped up and grinding with those new boys, I want to be wrapped up and grinding with Randy; Randolph Walker. That boy is so fine. Pot, do you think I'm going to hell because I want to kiss Randy?"*

"Naw girl;" Pot said, laughing. *"I pretend I'm kissing boys all the time. I know I ain't going to hell. Not only do I pretend I'm kissing them, I pretend I do it with them, too."*

"Ooh wee Pot," I said, *"you nasty girl. How can you say something nasty like that? I'll never do anything that nasty. To even think of doing something nasty like that turns my stomach."*

"I was just playing girl," Pot replied. *"I may look stupid, but I have lots of sense in this big head. As God is my witness Ann, I will never do the nasty."*

"Cross your heart and hope to die?" I challenged Pot.

"Yes." Pot said. (Pot put the tip of her finger to the tip of her tongue, crossed her heart, and raised her hand above her head as she said) *"Cross my heart and hope to die."*

1962 was a very good year for the girls and many other Black people. President John F. Kennedy was our new President; the Freedom Riders were making their way across the South; James Meredith was getting ready to attend the University of Mississippi; and Ann, Pot, and Jenny were getting ready to attend Junior High School. Mama Sara would say 1962 was a very good year.

Chapter 4

Wanting to fit in

The summer went by fast, and it was almost time for school to start. This was a new experience for me. I was excited about Junior High School, but the fear of going to a new school gave me an unpleasant feeling inside. I had many unanswered questions. Would there be students there like Bell Bellevue? Would my teachers like me? How would I be accepted by the boys?

I really liked boys, especially the ones with curly hair and pretty white teeth. But none of the boys really noticed me. I was hoping Junior High School would be a turning point in my life.

Mama Sarah took me and Pot school shopping. She could tell right off this was a change for us by the type of clothes we were choosing. She gave us that same ole run of the mill lecture she always gives.

"Ann and Pot," Mama Sarah said. *"I know y'all are about to go to a new school. And when you go, I want y'all to be young ladies, okay. Y'all don't have to prove anything to anybody. Just be yourself. Both of you have plenty of time to grow up. Y'all will be adults before you know it. So calm down and stay in control. Y'all hear me?"*

"*Yes ma'am*". Pot and I replied.

Pot and I did listen to Mama Sarah, but I don't think Mama Sarah realized that this was not an evening at the Mid-South Fair; this was Junior High School and we had to look the part.

"*No ma'am, Ann.*" Mama Sarah commented. "*You cannot get that skirt! First of all, it's too tight and I can see your under drawers right through the material.*"

"*But, Mama,*" I said. "*All the girls in Junior High School wear their skirts tight.*"

"*Good.*" Mama Sarah said. "*I'm glad you're going to Junior High School. You are a leader and all the girls can follow your lead. So pull that skin tight skirt off and try on this flair tailed one*".

"*And you too, Pot.*" Mama Sarah shouted. "*Get that tight skirt off your high tail behind and put this one on; right now! I'll be-damned.*" Mama Sarah said. "*If everybody at that school jumped in the lake, I guess y'all would act crazy and jump in the lake, too.*"

"*Mama Sarah is disgusting,*" I thought to myself, with a frown on my face.

We shopped all afternoon. When we got home, Aunt Kate said the outfits we picked were really cute. That remark from Aunt Kate made me feel better. I also appreciated Mama Sarah reminding me and Pot that we didn't have to prove anything to anybody. We are just as special as everyone else. That caused me to feel secure and a bit more relaxed.

A week later, Aunt Kate took me and Pot to the record shop. And low and behold, the Lord had answered my prayers! Jesus! Ms. Linda and Jenny were in the record shop. When Pot and I saw Jenny, we screamed out loud and ran to each other. We hugged for mercy. Pot and I were so happy to see Jenny alive and in the flesh.

Aunt Kate and Ms. Linda sat down and talked while we had a fun day choosing our favorite records. I loved the record shop. Collecting music was my hobby. I loved Rhythm & Blues, Doo-Wop, the Memphis Sound, Motown and everything in between. That day, I bought *Shop Around, Stubborn Kind of Fellow, Play Boy*, and *Hitch Hike*. Pot bought *You Beat Me to the Punch, Operator*, and *Soldier Boy*. Jenny had ten records and was still looking for more.

While Aunt Kate and Ms. Linda talked, catching up on the latest gossip; Pot, Jenny and I looked through hundreds of records, searching for that special record we could listen to for hours. As I searched I noticed this boy, about my age, in the store. He was so cute. He saw me looking at him and gave me a sexy smile. His teeth looked like the white keys on a Baby Grand piano and his hair was curly. He was the perfect height and he had broad shoulders. I could have screamed! He was so fine. Pot and Jenny were so busy looking through records they didn't even notice him. I said to myself, "*Good, I saw him first.*" For some reason, that day, I had to take a risk. This may have been out of character for me, but I had to ask him his name. This was the most daring act of bravery I had ever taken in my whole life. I walked over to him and said:

"*Hi,*"

"*Hi,*" the boy replied.

"*You live in this neighborhood*, I ask?"

"*Yea, do you?*" He responded.

"*Yes. My name is Ann. What's yours?*"

"*Willie Bill.*"

"*Well, Willie Bill, what kind of music are you looking for?*"

"*Nothing special,*" He said. "*Just something good I can add to my music collection.*"

"*I bet that's some music collection you have, huh?*"

"*Its okay;*" He said, "*could be better though. Who's your friend over there?*" He asked me.

When he asked me about my friend, I was crushed. For a moment, all kinds of negative thoughts about my self went through my mind. Am I ugly? Is my skin tone too dark? Is my hair nappy? Why doesn't he want to know me? I felt so small. But immediately, in my mind, I saw Mama Sarah's big brown eyes looking down on me. So, in my mind, I picked my self-esteem up, dusted my self-esteem off, and proceeded on.

"*Which one,*" I asked him. "*They're both my friends.*"

"*The one with the green ribbon in her hair,*" He said.

"*Oh, that's my friend Pottianna.*"

"*Pottianna;*" Willie Bill said. "*What a nice name.*"

He looked at Pot with that sly dog look in his eyes. I said to myself: *This no good Negro. I'm talking to him and he's looking at my friend. That's just like a no good Negro. Oh well, maybe I acted too hastily and made myself look like a fool.*

"You want to meet her?" I asked him.

"Sure, why not." He answered.

I had been yearning for a boy to like me, but Willie Bill let me know right off he wasn't the one. At least he was truthful. That meant a lot, so I took him over to meet Pot.

"Hey Pot," I said. *"Meet Willie Bill."*

Pot looked up from searching through the records. Her first look implied she liked him right off. I could see he liked her too.

"He's new to our neighborhood." I told Pot. *"So I introduced myself, and now I'm introducing him to you and Jenny."*

I don't think either of them heard a word I said. They were too engrossed in each other; they appeared to be in a hypnotic state of mind. I stood between them and snapped my fingers to get their attention. *"Snap. Snap."*

"Hey you two;" I said. *"Wake up and smell the coffee."* We all laughed. The introduction was nice and pleasant.

Willie Bill asked Pot if he could help her find some more music. Of course she said *"yes."* They talked until Aunt Kate

51

said it was time to go. Jenny thought Willie Bill was cute too. She said he may have a brother, cousin, or friend she and I could meet. I just looked at Jenny. She knew Deacon Johns wasn't going to let her meet nobody, nowhere, at no time. I wrote this day down as a very good day.

****

Willie Bill became friends with all of us. He made my and Pot's journey through Junior High School a pre-eminent delight. He was a couple of years older than we were, so he taught us a lot. We were newcomers to Junior High School and he was in his last year. And even better than that, when we get to High School, he could tell us all about it, and introduce us to all his nice friends. I could think of many ways Willie Bill could be an asset to us. He was a respectable guy, saying yes Sir, no Sir, yes Ma'am and no Ma'am to all our elders. His respect caused Mama Sarah and Ms. Polly Mae both to like him very much.

Mama Sarah and Ms. Mozella became friends with Willie Bill's mother. Mama Sarah would send her herbs and vegetables from our backyard garden and fruit from our fruit trees. Ms. Addie Mae was her name and Mr. Walter was her husband. Mr. Walter wasn't Willie Bill's father though. I overheard Ms. Mozella tell Mama Sarah that Ms. Addie Mae didn't know who Willie Bill's daddy was. Ms. Mozella said Ms. Addie Mae was in love with two men at the same time: Willie Russell and Bill Pryor. She said when Willie Bill was born, Ms. Addie Mae didn't know which one was the real father, and she didn't have the heart to choose. She wanted both of them to be his father. That's why she named her baby Willie Bill, after both of her lovers.

Ms. Mozella said both men wanted to marry Ms. Addie Mae, but after so much fighting and profane language between the two of them, she stopped speaking to both of them. Ms. Mozella said a year or two later, Mr. Walter came along, fell in love with Ms. Addie Mae, married her, and took care of her and Willie Bill too.

Ms. Addie Mae was a deep dark skinned beautiful woman. Mama Sarah said her ancestors came from New Orleans. Ms. Addie Mae had a strange dialect that sounded like French. I loved talking to her. She made me feel special and encouraged me to love myself. She often told me, *"Always remember Ann; there is beauty in all God's creations."*

Ms. Addie Mae was a woman of small stature and she could carry large baskets of clothes on her head. When she walked, her hips swayed from side to side like that of a belly dancer. I guess that's why so many men loved her. Willie Bill was her only child and she loved him very much.

Somehow, I believe God sent Willie Bill to me and Pot. He was our protector. He played football, basketball, and other sports, which projected real manhood. No one at school ever bullied or harassed us because Willie Bill was our friend.

However, in addition to all of his charm, Willie Bill did have his rough spots. He spoke and wrote in musical lyrics. He owned more records than one could count. I guess the lyrics in those songs had become a part of him. He would always express himself in the words of a song. Many times, I covered my hand over my mouth to keep from laughing. It was funny on one hand and very intriguing on the other. All his emotions were expressed in the words of a song. One day, as we walked home from school, I heard him tell Pot,

"Pottiana Love, I want you to know, it was just one look, and I fell so hard in love with you. Say you'll be mine forever. I thought I was dreaming, but I was wrong. But I'm gonna keep on dreaming until I make you my own."

Pot blushed. Her cheeks rose up like pomegranates. I believe Pot loved Willie Bill before she even knew what love really was.

Willie Bill had all the latest equipment to make music sound great. Large speakers, reel to reels and other devices to enhance the sound of his music collection. Ms. Addie Mae let him have backyard dances and the teenagers in our neighborhood would gather in their backyard for dance parties. A lot of teenagers fell in love from his collection of smooth slow jams.

Mama Sarah trusted Ms. Addie Mae to protect us and Ms. Addie Mae kept her eyes on everything going on. A few times, when Deacon Johns was out of town, Aunt Kate and Ms. Linda brought over baked brownies, hot dogs, and Kool-Aid to the dance for the children. Jenny would come too. The three of us, with the other children, would dance the night away. We would swing and dance to many good songs. Songs like, *Come See about Me*, *The Girl's All-right With Me*, *Pain in my Heart* and many other great songs. Willie Bill would always make, *Save the Last Dance for Me,* his last record before it was time to go home. He would make his way over to Pot and dance the last dance with her. I always slept peaceful after Willie Bill's dance parties. They were so much fun. This was the best life and I loved living it.

****

Willie Bill was Pot's and my guardian angel throughout Junior High School and that same protection reigned over us in High School. There was only one High School in our district, and by the Grace of God, Deacon Johns let Jenny attend. We were surprised that he didn't transport her across town to another private school like we thought he would. We counted our blessings and thanked God that we were all back together again.

Willie Bill schooled us on everything upon entering High School. Prejudice teachers, teachers who showed love and respect, and the bad students to stay away from. He was a very wise person and the number one person in his life, besides his mother, was Pot. He would do almost anything to make Pot laugh. Jenny and I benefitted from these pleasurable moments too. He reminded me of Mama Sarah in many ways. He was somewhat old fashioned and talked to us about books he had read. He had read many books. I don't know when he found the time. Maybe he read at night when everyone else was asleep like Mama Sarah does.

He was the first person to encourage me to try out to be a majorette. He said I had the perfect legs to be an excellent stepper. His encouragement inspired me so I practiced every day. I was not as pretty as some of the other girls, so I had to be the best; therefore, I practiced long and hard until I mastered all the routines to perfection.

Pot and Jenny said I was wasting my time, but Willie Bill believed I had a good chance to make the squad. He said I was the best he has ever seen. He encouraged me to at least try out, so I did.

A notice was posted at school for young ladies to tryout for a majorette. I entered my name. My moment came and my hard work paid off. I was the best performer of all the new prospects. Many students gave me a standing ovation. I was just that good! I believe I almost convinced Pot and Jenny; but, they knew just as I did, that performance was only one of the requirements the judges were looking for.

A week after the start of school, the names of the new majorettes were posted on the bulletin board in the gym. Pot, Jenny, and I rushed to the gym, excited and engaged with possibility. Nevertheless, my name was not on the list. I was crushed!

"How could they do this to me?" I said.

"*Man, I can't believe this;*" Jenny said. "*And you were really the best performer.*"

"*I'm not surprised,*" Pot said. "*You knew they were not going to pick you Ann. You know they don't pick dark skinned girls to be majorettes at this school! I don't know why you tried out in the first place! You know how unfair these gym teachers are! I can never understand why you always try to force your way through doors where you know you're not wanted! Mama Sarah always teaches us to only dwell where we are celebrated and appreciated! Being a majorette is no big deal anyway! Forget being a majorette and leave this phony shit alone!*" Pot was furious.

"*But Pot,*" I said. "*I was good! I was really good! I have to ask Ms. Hudson if I can be included with the finals. I have to ask her!*"

Ms. Hudson was the sponsor for the majorettes. Ann rushed down the hallway to her classroom. Pot and Jenny were shocked at what Ann was about to do, but they were too angry to stop her. Ann knew she was not selected because of her dark skin tone, but for some reason, she had to hear it from Ms. Hudson's lips. Ann knocked at Ms. Hudson's classroom door. "Knock; knock."

"*Come in*", Ms. Hudson replied.

Ann softly opened the door and stuck her head into the classroom.

"*Ms. Hudson,*" I said. "*May I speak with you for a minute?*"

"Yes, come in." Ms. Hudson replied. *"How may I help you?"*

By this time, Ann was teary-eyed and her voice trembled. She was very hurt. Ms. Hudson was an arrogant, egotistical Bitch with an excessive sense of self-importance; to blind to see for hate. She used her power and her position as a teacher to belittle many students and exaggerate her claim of being superior. She should have been diagnosed with NPD, Narcissistic Personality Disorder, and never given the opportunity to work with children. Ann tried to persuade Ms. Hudson to give her another chance, but Ms. Hudson wouldn't do it.

"Ms. Hudson," Ann asked in a trembling voice. *"I want to ask if I can be included as one of the finals for the new majorettes. Many of the students said I was really good, and I'm willing to practice long and hard. I have wanted to be a majorette my whole life! Can you please give me another chance?"*

"What did you say your name was?" Ms. Hudson asked.

"Sarah Foster," I answered.

"Well Miss Foster," Ms. Hudson said. *"To be a majorette at this school, you have to have it all, okay. It takes more than strong legs to be a majorette here. You get that? And do you see any Black girls on that majorette squad? Do you?*

"No ma'am."

"Okay Miss Foster," Ms. Hudson said. *"Stop wasting my time. I suggest that you get out of my classroom and close my door!"*

Ann stepped out of Ms. Hudson's classroom and slammed the door. Pot and Jenny were standing down the hall waiting, ready to help Ann get through this painful ordeal. But this time, Ann needed more than Pot and Jenny. She needed Mama Sarah. To hear a Black teacher, teaching at a Black school, ask one of the Black students "Do you see any Black girls on that majorette squad?" is devastating to that child. Something is wrong at that school and should be corrected immediately.

The girls walked home that afternoon depressed and unsure how to make the best of this bad situation. When Ann got home, Mama Sarah could see something was wrong by the way Ann slammed her books on the table.

"You have a good day at school, child?" Mama Sarah asked."

"Yes ma'am." I said.

Ann was somewhat reluctant about telling Mama Sarah what really happened at school that day. She didn't want Mama Sarah to think she was weak and had no backbone.

"Mama," I said to Mama Sarah. *"Why do people hate some people because their skin is dark? And why do our own people call each other black in a cruel and negative way. Why do we hate each other so? And why are we so unfair to each other?"* (Ann burst into tears.)

"What's wrong, baby?" Mama Sarah asked. *"Tell me what's wrong?"* (Mama Sarah was seriously concerned.)

(Whimpering, Ann said) *"I wanted to be a majorette at school, so I tried out. I did real well, but I was turned down because my skin tone is too dark."* (Ann burst into tears again.)

58

Mama Sarah pulled Ann over to her and sat Ann on her knee to comfort her. Mama Sarah made sure she handled this situation with love and care. She spoke to Ann in a very soft and caring voice.

"Now, now, darling, don't cry. I know you did well. I know whatever you do; you always give it your best. I'm so sorry this happened to you. Evidently those judges don't know very much about the History of the Black Man or the magnificent biochemistry of melanin. Sounds to me, like those judges need to read a few good books: Maybe books like, <u>The Miss Education of the Negro,</u> <u>The Philosophy and Opinions of Marcus Garvey,</u> *or a few good books on melanin. "My precious baby girl, thousands of people carry inferiority complexes with them all through life because some ignorant, uneducated, cold-hearted person destroyed their confidence. But Ann, my darling, we're not gonna let that happen to you. You are perfect! And never ever let anyone convince you to think that you're not. Not only are you perfect, but everybody is perfect, but most people don't believe they are. So, they can't be perfect because they don't believe it. Jesus taught us that, All Things Are Possible, if we would only believe. Believe Ann, and be the perfect person that you are."*

"I regret seeing our children suffer at the hands of immature, ignorant adults. This brainwashing tactic of skin color has caused phenomenal pain among Black folk in this country. Everything we have done to utterly destroy this giant has not worked. It still haunts us to this day. I guess God will have to send us another David." (Mama Sarah smiled as she went on to say):

"This skin color ordeal goes deep, Baby; too deep for most of us to understand. Many races struggle with this skin color monster, not just dark skinned Black folk. Light skinned Black

folk, Chinese, and even some White people. So, to get around all the hoopla about dark skin, people lighten their skin. For some reason, they tend to believe, the whiter the better. They use all kinds of bleaching creams and skin lighteners: Turmeric, Sandalwood, intravenous injections, and anything they can get their hands on to look whiter. I've often wondered, why! Granted, don't get me wrong. It's nothing wrong with a person lighting their skin, if that's what they want to do. It's their skin. But don't hate and discriminate because of a person's skin color. You're only hurting yourself with all that hate inside your soul. It shows that you're ignorant and uneducated. Be a better person than that."

"And as for you, young lady, never condemn yourself, and never condemn anyone else. Develop love for yourself and for all humanity; bring goodness into your life. As Black people, we must learn to control negative thoughts, and remove all this garbage from our minds, and learn to live Holy. We are a Holy nation of people, but we just don't know it. But, when good words are spoken from the mouth of Black people and Godly thoughts are in our mind, the Black man will soar like an eagle and rise above this state of barbaric conduct we have against one another."

"Black people have been pushed around and displaced so much until we are like salt that has lost its savor. We have been so divided until our high moral qualities and our superior state of being have almost been forgotten. And our ancestors, in this country, could see only what the Slave Master owned and very few things that the Black man owned. The Slave Master's thousands of acres of land, his beautiful mansion homes, his good food, his money, his servants, and everything anyone could ever wish for. Some of us loved the Slave Master, some of us didn't. And to this day, we are still divided. What we think governs our lives; and many bad things thought about Black people are believed to be true. Many of those things are not true. They are only bad thoughts entered into

the Universe, manifesting bad things to manifest in Black folk lives."

"So, until this great change for Black people become a reality, you, Miss Ann, (Mama Sarah said, pointing her finger and touching Ann's nose), *"Always think positive thoughts about yourself and everyone else. Speak good positive words and look for the good in people. This will bring good into your own life. Our words have power and life within them. Every time we speak, we are using power, whether that power is good or whether that power is bad. Never, ever, criticize anyone. Always give appreciation, hope and encouragement. You understand Ann?"*

"Yes ma'am, Mama."

Mama Sarah went on and on, that day, explaining to Ann how Black people have been divided and brainwashed for many years. How they have been used and abused and hated for no legitimate reason. How fear, distrust and envy is the major cause of the fall of the Black race in this country. Throughout Ann's life, she always remembered that conversation. But, it was hard for Ann to understand how Ms. Hudson, being a teacher, and a college graduate, didn't know simple things like Mama Sarah knew. From that day on Ann was never intimidated by her skin tone ever again. When she heard negative words spoken about Black people, especially by Black people, Ann knew there was a fear inside of them. A fear of inadequacy and a need to pull someone down to make themselves look big. Ann prayed they would someday grow strong, recover, and overcome their fears.

Chapter 5

Hurt can last forever

I soon found it in my heart to forgive Ms. Hudson and moved on to enjoy my high school years. There were many other activities Pot, Jenny and I participated in that brought happiness and were very satisfying. We joined one of the clubs at our school and worked with our school newspaper staff. We also sang in our high school choir and participated in many performances across the Mid-South.

In late May, 1966, the end of our tenth grade year, Willie Bill was graduating high school. High School graduation was a grand occasion in our community. Over three hundred seniors were graduating; some by a narrow margin and others, like Willie Bill, with honors. I was so happy for them. The good thing about it was our high school choir was singing at the graduation. Pot, Jenny, and I sang our hearts out.

It was hard to believe how fast time had passed. Many of the children in our neighborhood had become young adults. My two brothers had graduated high school and were attending college in Washington, D. C. Ms. Addie Mae couldn't afford college for Willie Bill so he volunteered for the Army. He had decided to serve three years in the military and pay for college by way of the G. I. Bill. He had orders to report to Fort Bragg, North Carolina U.S. Army Military Base two weeks after graduating high school.

Growing up was finally becoming a reality for many of us. But I must say; we have many wonderful memories to recall. The dances in Willie Bill's back yard and all the reckless mischief Pot, Jenny and I got into. I will cherish those memories forever. When I think of those happy times, all I can do is smile.

As soon as Willie Bill reached Fort Bragg, he wrote Pot a letter almost every day. Willie Bill still expressed himself, or wrapped as the hip boys called it, by using the lyrics from a song. Pot would let me and Jenny read the letters and we would laugh our behinds off.

Willie Bill's letters were crazy. He would end his letters by telling Pot: "*Save the Last dance for me.*" Pot was the happiest girl in the world. She truly believed Willie Bill loved her and she loved him just as much. He sent Pot lots of pictures and she cherished those pictures and his letters as if they were gold nuggets from heaven. I told Pot she was so lucky to have a special guy, who has his head on straight, who's smart, and who writes crazy love letters to make her laugh. In one of his letters he said to Pot:

"*Alone from night to night you'll find me;*
 too weak to break the chains that bind me;
 I need no shackles to remind me;
 I'm just a prisoner of your love."

"*You're in my dreams, awake or sleeping,*
 upon my knees to you I'm creeping.
 My very life is in your keeping,
 I'm just a prisoner of your love."

Pot would sleep with Willie Bill's letters under the mattress on her bed. She said it made her feel he was right there in bed next to her. I knew they were meant for each other the moment I saw them together. No matter how many boys tried to date Pot, Willie

Bill had no fear. He knew Pot was his, all his and his alone. Pot felt the same for him. I knew they would marry someday and I looked forward to being in their wedding.

Before Willie Bill was gone six months, many of his so called friends tried to rap on Pot. Pot was a very pretty girl and many of Willie Bill's backstabbing "fake friends" wanted her. Pot almost looked White. Her physique was one that women would kill for and her legs were almost as pretty as mine.

The boys liked Jenny too, but they never said anything to her. Jenny was skinny, straight up and down, with no curves anywhere. She had more socks and tissue paper in her bra than tits. But more than that, they were afraid of Deacon Johns. The children at school and in our neighborhood referred to Deacon Johns as the Count, as in "*Count Dracula*". And me, well the boys liked me too, but, who would choose me over Pot and Jenny. Yes, I was cute and one of the most attractive girls in our neighborhood, but they couldn't see me for looking at Pot and Jenny's long hair and light skin. I wasn't mad at them though, because what they liked in girls, I liked those same characteristics in boys: light skin, a nice fresh hair cut, a well-toned physique, and light brown eyes. But more than anything else, the boys were afraid of Mama Sarah too. Mama Sarah taught me, Pot, and Jenny well. She taught us to keep out dresses down and keep our grades up and that was no aphorism; that was the law.

However, there was this one boy, Marvin Young, who had his eyes on Pot. The boys in our neighborhood referred to him as Marvelous Marvin. When they called his name, they had a great big grin on their face as if they were addressing The Great Hannibal Barca himself. Why, I don't know. He wasn't cute and he dropped out of school in the 9th grade. If you want to ask me, he was a heel, a despicable unscrupulous heel. I guess all the guys liked him because he had a reputation of having lots of girls. He had a car, nice clothes, and money. When he stopped in at the malt shop to get his shoes shined he always tipped the shoe shine boy a dollar bill. That small gesture made him shine like royalty.

The word in the neighborhood was that his mother had run off with a much younger man and his daddy didn't care what he did. The kids said most of his dad's time was spent away from home working and chasing women. I guess you can say Marvelous Marvin was on his own, doing whatever he wanted to do, and this lifestyle gained him lots of friends. Many young boys thought this was the life and made Marvin's house the hangout spot in the hood.

Pot was so hot and fast. She thought being naughty was cute and would make people like you. I didn't think it was cute at all; I thought it was stupid. Pot would blush and sparkle with joy every time Marvin spoke to us. He would flirt and wink his eye at us and Pot's cheeks would blush tomato red. I couldn't stand Marvin. I knew he was up to no good. Pot knew it too, but Miss hot mama Pot, loved that attention.

When Pot turned sixteen, Ms. Polly Mae said she could receive company. Mama Sarah said I had to wait until I was eighteen. No matter how you look at it, her decision was final. Nevertheless, every young guy in our neighborhood wanted to call on Pot. But being Willie Bill's girl and having me and Jenny standing guard, all the boys got the message and went their way. Jenny and I were there to make sure Pot stayed Willie Bill's girl.

****

Willie Bill would occasionally come home on leave from the Army. He looked very handsome in his Army uniform. He had so much to tell about his travels at home and over seas. He told Pot they would be married some day and he would take her to all the places he had been. He told me and Jenny he told his Army buddies about us, and they were looking forward to meeting us. Willie Bill showed us pictures of them, and he took pictures of us to show his buddies.

Aunt Kate would take us many places when Willie Bill was home: To the movies, on Beale Street, Fuller Park, and The Fairgrounds. I loved riding The Pippin Roller Coaster and The Grand Carousel. We would go to H. Salt Fish and Chips, the Harlem House and many other nice restaurants across the City. I loved eating Hotdog Specials and Salisbury steak dinners from the Harlem House. Aunt Kate was proud of Willie Bill. She treated him like he was her own son. When it was time for him to return to his military duties, Aunt Kate and Big Daddy would take him to the airport for a happy send off with all his friends by his side.

When Willie Bill was on a long military assignments Pot would become lonely and sad. I had to do everything I could think of, to uplift her Spirit. One evening, just before dusk, I suggested that we walk up the street and get a burger and shake from Mr. Harthorn's Malt Shop. I thought the loud music from the café across the street and people standing all around enjoying themselves would give Pot a boost. Mama Sarah said it was okay as long as we behaved ourselves and act like the ladies she taught us to be. Pot and I also decided, on our way back, if Deacon Johns wasn't home and it was okay with Ms. Linda, we would stop and sit on the porch and talk with Jenny for a while. In essence, we had planned a wonderful evening I knew would put Pot in a better mood.

Just before getting to the window to order our burger and shake, Marvin drove up in his white convertible with the top laid back. He was looking at Pot as if he wanted to do something freaky to her. He was eyeing her skin tight shorts, looking right between her legs. Pot, with her stupid butt, was tickled pink. He beckoned his head to summon Pot. She strolled over to his car like a two bit harlot from the back woods of Georgia. I stood there, looking at her. I couldn't believe my eyes. I said to myself, *"What in the hell is wrong with this fool? Is she crazy or what?"* He said something to Pot that made her laugh, so I did give him a plus for that. I called to Pot to get her attention.

"Come on Pot." I said to her. *"We've got to hurry so we can get back."*

"Okay, wait a minute." Pot said, leaning over on Marvin's car.

I stood there waiting impatiently, while Marvin conned Pot into riding with him. Something in my Spirit made me feel this wasn't a good idea, but I didn't listen.

"Ann," Pot said. *"Marvin wants us to ride with him for a minute. He wants to show us where he lives and introduce us to a couple of his friends."*

"I don't know about that Pot." I said. *"We've got to get back."*

"He's going to bring us right back. He says he only lives about five minutes from here. Come on Ann…. It's okay."

I didn't feel good about it at all. But when I looked at Pot and she looked so happy, I hoped it would be okay. I went with them. Pot got in the front seat with Marvin and I got in the back. Marvin took off speeding, leaving a long trail of black smoke behind us. I couldn't believe I let Pot talk me in to this. I felt so stupid. I guess my negative energy landed right smack on his cerebral cortex. He started to pick at me.

"Hey lady back there," Marvin said to me, *"Pretty lady."*

I looked at him in his rearview mirror with a frown on my face.

"Why yo jaws always so tight" Marvin asked me. *"You scared of me or something? I don't bite!"*

I looked at him and rolled my eyes. *"Can you please turn that loud music down?"* I asked him.

Pot looked back, looking at me, laughing. That stupid Marvin turned the music up louder like a fool. I was really a little scared. I knew if Mama Sarah knew we were in the car with this fool, she would kill us. Plus, it was getting dark. I wanted to jump out of that car and run home.

After the short drive, we pulled up to Marvin's house and parked. You could hear music coming from the inside of the house. His house was on a steep hill with a flight of about twenty concrete steps leading to the front porch. The exterior green paint on the house was dull and peeling.

The ceiling on the porch was sagging from the weight of a leaky roof and pieces of the ceiling were hanging, waiting to fall on somebody's head. Two young guys were sitting on a rusty swing on the front porch. They greeted Marvin with a crazy handshake I had never seen before. They were dusty looking fellows who needed to comb their hair and probably needed a bath too.

The door screen on the front door was torn to pieces and instead of opening the screen door, Marvin just stepped through the torn screen in the door. Pot and I, like two little pick-a-ninnies, stepped through the torn screen right behind him.

The small shotgun house was dark with a broken down sofa in each corner of the living room. Six guys were sitting around just hanging out. One guy had a chain in his hand, holding onto a thirty pound Doberman.

Marvin introduced us, and referred to Pot as his lady and to me as Pot's friend. He said we were there to hang out for a while and have a little fun. I was so scared. I was holding my legs together, tight, to hold my pee. I swallowed my spit and I think my whole throat went down with it. All I could see was the coroner carrying me and Pot down those steps. Mama Sarah said everybody has a guardian angel that's always with them. I was hoping my guardian angel was with me, working on a way for me and Pot to get the hell out of there.

Marvin told two of the guys to get up and give me and Pot a seat. Pot and I sat down side by side. I could feel Pot was just as afraid as I was. Marvin went to the kitchen and came back drinking a beer. He sat down between me and Pot and tried to get Pot to drink some of the beer, but she turned her head. The music was blasting. Marvin pulled Pot from the sofa and started to slow dance with her, grinding at the hips as if his hormones were raging. One of the guys asked me to slow dance too. I was too afraid to tell him no. So I danced. We slow danced again and again. After the third record ended, Marvin took Pot by her hand and headed toward one of the bedrooms. Out of nowhere, these words came out of my mouth:

"Marvin," I said. *"Can Pot show me where your bathroom is before y'all go back there?"*

He looked at me as if he wanted to strangle me and told Pot the bathroom was in the back on the left. We hurried back to the bathroom and I locked the door.

"Pot," I said. *"I'm so scared. Please don't go to that back room with that boy. If you do, I know those other boys are going to rape me. I know they will Pot. I know they will!"*

I was almost hysterical. Pot started to shake me; she told me to hush-up and listen.

"I'm scared too," Pot said. *"But, we've got to get out of here."*

Tears started to run down my face. Pot told me to hush-up and listen for a minute. She stood on the commode seat to see if we could get out of the bathroom window. She said the window was not too high and I could jump from the window to the ground. Pot told me to run to the second house, run out to the street, run home, and don't stop until I get to Mama Sarah.

"But Pot," I said. *"I can't leave you by yourself. Let's go together. Both of us,"* I begged her.

"No," Pot said. *"We can't do that. Once they know we're gone, they'll come after us and sic that dog on us. So listen and do as I say. I can't let all those boys mess with you. You're a virgin. So listen to me! I'm going to pull my shorts up, pull my top off my shoulders, and wrap this towel around me. They'll think I'm naked and that'll stall them until you get away."*

"Oh Pot," I said. *"They'll really rape you then, and you're a virgin too."* Tears ran down my face.

"No they won't." Pot said. *"Marvin's not going to let them mess with me. You just do as I say. I'm not a virgin, let me handle this."*

At that same time, Marvin called to Pot! She answered immediately.

"Okay Baby." Pot said to him. *"Just one minute."*

Pot and I hugged real tight and she helped me get through the window. As I jumped to the ground and started to run, I could hear all the guys marvel, whistle, and applaud. I guess they really did think Pot was naked. But I did as Pot said, I ran as fast as I could.

I ran until I was out of breath and my run turned into a very fast walk. Shortly before I made it to our neck of the woods, Marvin's car pulled up beside me. Pot got out and ran to where I was. Marvin made a U-turn in the middle of the street and went back the other way. I was shaking with fear. I grabbed Pot by the shoulders and asked her what happened. Pot looked at me and burst into laugher. She said when she came out of the bathroom those boys thought she was really naked and they went wild. She said Marvin took her to his bedroom. Pot said, before anything sexually happened, she immediately told him I was so scared that I jumped out of the bathroom window and was running home to get my grandmother and come back to his house with the police. She said Marvin didn't want to hear that. Pot said he told her to get dressed and they were rushing to catch me before I got home. Pot said he went for the whole story, hook, line, and sinker. Pot said she told him she would give him some next time. Pot was laughing so hard. I sighed, took a long deep breath and said, *"Thank you, Jesus."*

I kept thinking about Pot saying she wasn't a virgin and wondered how could that be. She would have told me if something happened between her and Willie Bill. Maybe she just said that to make me go through that window and do what she told me to do. Anyway, I was so glad we got out of that situation safe until that's all I could think about at that time. Pot and I happily sashayed our little behinds on home and never got in the car with Marvin again.

The next day, Pot and I told Jenny about our little dangerous escapade. It was so funny and we had a good laugh. Jenny told us this little adventure should let us know it's time to put foolish things aside and look forward to graduation.

Jenny was right. Graduation was closer than we realized. So we all decided to get busy and concentrate on graduating high school.

Next year would be a big year for us: Our high school prom, class day, and that great walk across the stage to get our high school diplomas; then college, a quantum leap for us.

And speaking of college; news spread fast in our neighborhood. The neighbors were all-ready saying Deacon Johns had talked to someone in Nashville and Jenny was going to Vanderbilt Medical School to become a doctor. My mom and dad told Mama Sarah they wanted me to go to college in Detroit. A scholarship fund on my dad's job would pay a large portion of my college tuition. I hated to hear that. If I had to go to college in Detroit, I just wouldn't go to college at all. Pot, Jenny, and I talked about college all the time. Our greatest fear was that we would be separated again. We couldn't let that happen. We had to think of a plan, quick, before it was too late.

Jenny was a genius at planning and coming up with good ideas. She would sit around Deacon Johns and learn everything from him. Jenny said sometimes she would pretend to be asleep, to hear Deacon Johns and his gangster friends organize and plan how to run things in the Black community. Jenny learned a lot. She became an expert at signing Deacon Johns' name and could swindle her way out of any heist and cover her tracks well. She told me and Pot to leave everything to her. Jenny said all three of us would go to college and all three of us would graduate.

****

For the next several months, we put all foolish things aside and focused on our future. We worked as junior ushers in our church and worked with the yearbook staff at our school. We kept ourselves busy days, nights, and weekends too.

Pot wrote Willie Bill often, telling him everything we were involved in. Jenny and I day dreamed about meeting his handsome Army buddies someday.

Our junior year of high school was winding down. We had made quite a name for ourselves. Our grades were good and neither of us was pregnant, which was a milestone in our community. To my knowledge, we were all still virgins regardless of what went down at Marvin's house.

Deacon Johns was even nice to me and Pot every once in a while. He even asked Jenny to ask me and Pot to help with our church picnic. We were suspicious of the change in his behavior, but we still worked hard to make the picnic a success, and it was.

That same night after the picnic, I could hardly sleep. I tossed and turned all night long. I thought I would sleep well after having such a good time, but I guess I ate too many hotdogs. The next morning I got up early. That was the first time in my whole life I had seen the sun come up. It was so bright and warm. It made me feel good. I got a bowl of cereal, sat on the front porch and enjoyed the warmth of the morning sun.

I wasn't the only early riser though. I looked up the street and saw a blue car stop in front of Ms. Addie Mae's house. I was surprised to see someone going to their house so early in the morning. Two White men got out of the car dressed in Army uniforms. I stood up to get a better look. My mind was puzzled, wondering why those men were there.

After knocking on Ms. Addie Mae's door, someone let them in. I stood there, on our porch, wondering what was going on. A few minutes later, I heard a wailing cry come from Ms. Addie's house. I ran in the house to throw on some clothes so I could walk up there. I knew something had happened. While getting dressed, I knocked over my alarm clock and woke Mama Sarah up.

"Ann," Mama Sarah yelled. *"What're you doing in there? What are you knocking over this early in the morning?"*

"My *alarm clock Mama, I'm sorry."* I then went into Mama Sarah's bedroom.

"Mama, I believe something has happened."

"What do you mean, you believe something has happened?"

"Two White men just went over Ms. Addie Mae's house and they had Army uniforms on."

"Oh Lord." Mama Sarah said. *"I hope nothing has happened to that boy. Lord, it'll kill Addie Mae."* Mama Sarah hurried out of bed and started to get dressed too.

"I'm putting some clothes on," I told Mama Sarah, *"so I can run around there and get Pot."*

I tied my shoes, jumped off the porch, and ran to the Back Alley to Pot's house. Pot was still asleep, so I knocked on her bedroom window to wake her up. *(Knock. Knock)*

"Pot, Pot, wake up. Pot, wake up."

Pot raised her bedroom window to see what I wanted.

75

"Ann, what you want? "Where're you going this early in the morning?"

"Pot" I said. *"I think something's going on with Willie Bill."*

"Why you say that?" Pot asked, surprisingly curious.

"There're two White men over Ms. Addie Mae's house, and they have on Army uniforms."

"Oh my God" Pot screamed! *"I hope Willie Bill is okay!"*

Pot was up and dressed in a few minutes. We hurried to Ms. Addie Mae's house. But before we made it there, an ambulance drove up to her door. The sound of the ambulance caused many neighbors to crowd around to see what was going on.

The ambulance attendants brought Ms. Addie Mae out on a stretcher and put her in the ambulance. She was wailing helplessly in agony and distress. Pot and I knew something horrible had happened. Mama Sarah came from Ms. Addie Mae's house over to where Pot and I were standing.

"He's gone y'all." Mama Sarah said. *"The Army Sergeant said Willie Bill was killed in Vietnam."*

Pot turned and started to run. I ran after her, shouting, asking her to wait. She didn't stop until she was home. She stopped at the porch, sat down, covered her face with her hands, and wailed. I felt so much pain for her.

"Pot, I'm so sorry." I said to her. *"I'm so sorry, Pot."*

Pot leaned on my shoulder as she cried, saying:

"Ann, he can't be dead! He's just a boy, Ann. He's just a boy! Oh Ann, I love him so much! I love him, Ann. I love him! What am I going to do? What am I going to do?" Pot cried so hard.

I put my arm around Pot to comfort her. Her tears poured like rain. I couldn't help but cry with her. Pot said she would never love anyone else. She said she would always love Willie Bill, and no one would ever take his place. Pot said her heart would belong to Willie Bill forever. She said she would always love him and only him, and I believed her. I truly believed her!

The Vietnam War saw the highest proportion of Blacks ever to serve in an American war. During the height of the United States involvement, from 1965 through 1969, Blacks who formed eleven percent of the population in the United States made up 12.6 percent of the soldiers in Vietnam. The majority of these were in the infantry, and although authorities differ on the figures, the percentage of Black combat fatalities during that period was a staggering 14.9 percent.

Chapter 6

Trying to put the pieces together

Willie Bill's death was very painful for everyone. The whole neighborhood grieved. It was hard to understand how something so bad could happen to someone so good. Mama Sarah worked hard to comfort everyone the best she knew how. Her words of wisdom, her prayers, and her Godly touch were comforting to Ms. Addie Mae and Pot, but it just wasn't enough.

Ms. Addie Mae became under the care of a doctor and had to take medication to sleep at night. The neighbors constantly prayed for her and the church lifted her up in prayer too. Pot was also very broken. She was like a person I didn't know anymore. She hated herself. She blamed herself for telling Willie Bill she thought volunteering for the Army was a great idea. She expressed to me that she wasn't worthy of anybody's love, not even God's love. And as the weeks passed, Pot turned into something ugly. She didn't care about herself anymore. I had to remind her from time to time she needed to take a bath. She tried smoking cigarettes, and her libido was uncontrollable. And to every guy who asked, she said yes. Pot needed help and Jenny and I did everything we could to help her through this crisis. We were there for her and would never leave. We tried to hide all this stuff from Mama Sarah and Ms. Polly Mae, and with God's help, I believe we did.

As time passed, things were gradually getting back to normal. We would see Ms. Addie Mae and Mr. Walter sitting on the front porch from time to time, but Ms. Addie Mae was never active and outgoing like she was before. Mr. Walter eventually talked her into moving out of that house to rid her of all those hurtful memories. They bought a small house on a few acres of land in Collierville, Tennessee, for a change of surroundings. We all hated to see them go, but we knew this change was the best thing to happen for Ms. Addie Mae.

Things didn't go as well for Pot. I don't think she'll ever get over Willie Bill. He meant more to her than anyone could have dreamed of; and letting go for Pot was hell. Her source of comfort was not in me, Jenny, nor her mom. It was in her dance. She would lose herself in her dance, especially to records Willie Bill loved. Pot would listen to Willie Bill's favorite records and dance alone all day by herself. Although it seemed a bit abnormal, it helped her situation for the moment and led to a good nights sleep. I knew in my heart that someway and somehow, time would heal her wounded heart, and Jenny and I would be right there to see her through.

****

Finally, the holidays came and Christmas brought a little happiness to cheer our hearts. However, a few weeks later, so many dreadful things were going on in Memphis, until personal lives were put on the back burner. Our city was virtually falling apart. This was due to a work strike between the City of Memphis and our Sanitation workers. Our city was turned upside down and extreme confusion was everywhere: Boycotts, picketing, thousands of marching protestors, and tons of stinky garbage scattered all over our streets. Amidst all the chaos, The White House Federal troops and the National Guard were summoned to maintain peace and order. A dusk to dawn curfew was imposed and many residents were fearful of leaving their homes. My mom and dad talked about coming to Memphis to take us back to Detroit with them. They didn't want any harm to come to us. But Mama Sarah assured them, that everything at our house was okay and we were safe. Nonetheless, the chaos didn't cease; it escalated. Things got so ugly in Memphis until it brought Dr. Martin Luther King Jr. to town.

Mama Sarah had very high regards for Dr. King. All his works were a part of her library. She talked about him like he was part of our family. When he was in Memphis, her eyes were glued to the television set day and night. Many of his works were added to the wallpaper in our bathroom. And I was so pleased to see Mama Sarah so happy about Dr. King being right here in our own town. It led to a lot of good conversation for Mama Sarah and Ms. Mozella. Mama Sarah believed Dr. King came to uphold what's right and just for all God's children.

I could see The Spirit of God in Dr. King's eyes as he worked hard to bring peace and justice to a city in turmoil. And, on Thursday, April 4, 1968, right here in Memphis, a group of ungrateful, good-for-nothing bastards murdered Dr. King! Assassinated him! Took his life! A senseless act perpetrated by a group of evil; vicious, inhumane human beings, corrupted enough to destroy their own mothers. I wish Dr. King had never come to Memphis!

For a short while, I hated this city and was ashamed to live here. I even considered going to Detroit. The smell of rotten, stinking garbage was exactly what this city deserved. And all those lowlife murderous rats who laid in wait to kill Dr. King should burn in hell!

All the wind was taken out of Mama Sarah. She wasn't her old self at all. She was very quiet, she read a lot, and stood silently at our back door each evening, watching the sun go down. Sometimes, I would stand beside her, put my arm around her waist, and watch the sun go down standing by her side. And, I didn't say a word.

After the shock and heartbreak of Dr. King's death, Memphis tried hard to pick herself up and move forward again. But Memphis will probably forever bow her head in shame for this horrible act. To renew and stand strong again, Memphis must repent for all her dirt, turn from her evil ways, and blossom into a new life of fairness and justice for all its citizens. Dr. King's children should be compensated and a formal apology should be given for Dr. King's life being taken in this City. Memphis will then stand strong, feel proud and rise in this Great Nation, with honor, respect and peace once again. Hold your head up Memphis, you will rise to the top again.

****

A few weeks later, Aunt Kate called me, Pot, and Jenny together. She asked us not to talk about anything negative, or unhappy in the presence of Mama Sarah. Aunt Kate asked us to talk about good and happy things, filled with lots of laughter, to make Mama Sarah feel better. Jenny suggested since we were graduating High School we should talk about college. Maybe that would redirect Mama Sarah's mind in another direction and move her on from thinking about the death of Dr. King. We all thought it was a splendid idea.

When we started to talk about college, the idea snowballed. Everybody was talking about college. The people in our neighborhood, students at school, people at church, everybody. I guess we really stirred up controversy with that idea. Many people thought we were crazy though. College! How were we going to pay for it? Jenny's family had money, but as for me and Pot, going to college was a pipe dream. We had no money and neither of us was aware of the necessary requirements needed for a person to be admitted to college.

A few days later, I went with Mama Sarah to take Deacon Johns his freshly ironed shirts. We entered their home with a happy good morning greeting, hoping to find Deacon Johns in a very good mood.

"Good morning y'all," Mama Sarah said to Deacon Johns and Ms. Linda.

"I'm bringing your shirts for the week, Sir." Mama Sarah told Deacon Johns. *"I'll be bringing y'all sheets and towels later today."*

"And, oh, by the way Deacon Johns, Sir," Mama Sarah said. *"I wanted to ask if you can help me get Ann and Pot into a local Junior College or Trade School after they graduate high school.*

"A Junior College or Trade School," Deacon Johns replied. *"That's going to be tough."*

"That can be costly too." Deacon Johns said. *"Jenny is going to Vanderbilt to become a medical doctor and it's costing me an arm and a leg. I can't make any promises, but, if I have time, I'll see if I can look into it for you."*

"Yes Sir. Thank you Deacon."

Mama Sarah knew all along Deacon Johns wasn't serious about helping her get the girls in school. She was a little worried so she decided Ann may have to go to Detroit so her parents can send her to school. Mark and Ben were in college and doing well. They were going to be Engineers. The College Funding Committee on Charlie Murphy's job helped the boys get into college and was paying their tuition. Ann didn't want

to hear anything about Detroit. She immediately became unhappy and depressed.

"Mama," Ann shouted. *"I don't want to go up there! I don't know anybody in Detroit. I hate going up there! Every time I go up there, I get sick. What do you want Mama? You want me to get sick and die?"*

"Shut your mouth Ann!" Mama Sarah screamed at Ann. *"Stop acting a fool. You know you don't use words like sick and dying. Those are not words of the Lord! If I hear those words come out of your mouth again, I will shake the shit out of you. You hear me Ann! I'll shake the shit out of you! And I mean it!"*

Mama Sarah believed words were life and very powerful. She believed you could speak things into being with the words that come out of your mouth, just as God spoke the world and everything that's very good into being.

Ann ran from the kitchen to the front porch sobbing and crying. Mama Sarah got her switch off top of the refrigerator that had laid there for years, and started out after Ann. Kate intervened, hoping Mama Sarah would understand Ann's frustrations and reconsider.

"Mama," Kate shouted, *"Leave her alone! You know she don't want to leave you. Calm down. We'll think of something. Amy Mae and Charlie Murphy have enough on their hands. They're starving and going ragged trying to send those boys to school. We'll go in prayer and our God will work it out."*

****

The next day, after Sunday school, I told Pot and Jenny about my run in with Mama Sarah. I told them I was planning to run away. I said Mama Sarah was mean and was planning to send me to Detroit after graduation, and I wasn't going. This unhappy feeling of separation wasn't good for us. You could see it in all three of our eyes. We had to do something and do it fast.

"Let's not panic." Jenny said. *"Let me think. We have to come up with a plan. Graduation is only a few weeks away, so we have to do something fast. Daddy has several letters on his desk about college scholarships from colleges all over Tennessee. I'll look through them and see what I can come up with."*

"What do you mean?" I asked Jenny.

"I mean, I'm not going to Nashville by myself." Jenny replied. *"I'm taking my two best friends with me. Right now, I don't know how I'll do it, but I'll think of something. Just leave everything to me, and watch my superhuman brain go to work. Believe me; I'll come up with something."*

We jumped for joy. Danced a little jig and headed back into church for Sunday services. I didn't know what to think of Jenny's little magical incantations and Pot didn't care. Pot just wanted to get out of Memphis. After Willie Bill died, she tried hard to engulf herself in dancing and sex. Trying to rid her self of his memory, but it wasn't working, so Pot just wanted to get the hell out of Dodge. And Jenny, sometimes I couldn't figure her out. Deacon Johns was not her real true father, but she was just like him. She could scheme and lie with a straight face and people would actually believe her. She was a pro at deceit, but her Spirit was loving and kind. When we were children, Jenny would steal checks out of Deacon Johns' checkbook, sign Deacon Johns' name and Mr. Perry, the owner of the corner store, thought the signature was authentic. Pot and I would wait on the outside of the store and Jenny would come out with everything: candy, drinks, toys, rag boloney, crackers, and many other goodies. Deacon Johns never fathomed that Jenny would do such a thing. But as for college, I was praying Jenny wouldn't do something foolish and get us all in trouble. My fingers were crossed every day.

****

The next few weeks went by fast. Before the girls knew it, they were marching to Pomp and Circumstance, graduating High School. Everything was so beautiful. A sea of white: Three hundred graduates ready to start a new beginning.

I was so happy to graduate high school. Everybody came to our graduation. My Mom, Dad, my brothers, everyone from church and the whole neighborhood. Aunt Kate gave me and Pot a grand reception. We had everything to eat; white tablecloths were on the tables and the centerpieces were beautiful vases filled with live flowers. We had punch and cake, and the music was very nice. Mama Sarah said no dancing though; it was Sunday, so we had to show the Lord respect. June 2, 1968 was the happiest day of my life.

The following Tuesday, my mom, dad, and brothers were all packed up and ready to head back north. I was so glad to see them go. I was hoping they would leave before plans of furthering my education came up. Nobody asked any questions and I didn't say a word about my plans for my future. When their car pulled off, I was counting the hours for my family to make it back to Detroit.

I would have washed dishes at the Greyhound bus station before going to Detroit. I don't know why I didn't like Detroit. I hated going up there and I had no idea why I didn't like it.

Now that everything was over and everybody was gone, there was mostly silence in our house. The only sounds came from the TV and the radio. I didn't know what to do, or say. What was next for me and Pot? Did I make a mistake by not going back with my parents? Jenny had it made and I was happy for her, but Pot and I were walking around with a big fat question mark in our heads.

So, for the next several weeks, I could hardly sleep. I tossed and turned every night, trying not to worry about my future. I didn't want to ask Mama Sarah and Aunt Kate for money for college; that wouldn't be fair to them. I didn't want to bring up the Army. I know Mama Sarah wouldn't go for that. I didn't have a job, and it was the last week of July. I was stuck.

But, the first week of August, I'll be damned. I don't know how the hell Jenny pulled this thing off, but she did. Jenny got me and Pot a full, four year Scholarship to a State College in Nashville, Tennessee. The Scholarship was from the same Foundation that funded Jenny's Scholarship. Jenny did a lot of copying and pasting and signing Deacon Johns' name. Deacon Johns was very well known by the Board of Directors for this Scholarship Foundation. The Scholarship paid the recipient's tuition, paid for their books, housing, and other student needs. The Scholarship was legal, and funded for four full years. If Deacon Johns had known, he would have choked the shit out of Jenny.

I was coming out of the bathroom when Aunt Kate was coming from the mailbox with the letter in her hand. She stopped at the kitchen table and immediately opened the letter addressed to me from a college in Nashville.

"What are you doing getting mail from a college in Nashville Ann?" Aunt Kate asked.

"Me? I don't know." I said. *"What does it say?"* Aunt Kate began to read the letter and almost fainted.

"Mama, Mama!" Aunt Kate called to Mama Sarah. *"Come here, you've got to see this."*

Mama Sarah came running. *"What's the matter with you?"*

"Read this." Aunt Kate said.

Mama Sarah took the letter and began reading. At that point, I didn't know what to think. I was scared as hell. My heart was pounding like a drum. All of a sudden, Mama Sarah let out a loud holler and started shouting. I was stunned.

"Oh Lord," Mama Sarah shouted! *"Thank you, Jesus. My prayers have been answered! Oh yes, Lord. I praise your Holy Name!"*

"Mama, what does the letter say?" I asked.

"You're going to college, Anna Two! You're going to college too! The Lord has answered my prayers. God has opened another door for you and I thank Him."

At that very same moment, Pot came running through the door with the same identical letter in her hand, addressed to her. Everyone was so grateful! Mama Sarah shouted with joy.

"I know Deacon Johns though this was his chance to keep y'all apart." Mama Sarah said. *"He may be a deacon of the church,*

but I don't think he knows that, "with God All Things are Possible!"

Nothing can keep the three of you apart, Anna Two. You, Pot, and Jenny are like the Petals of a Three-Leafed Clover! Nothing can keep y'all apart. I'm so happy for y'all! Hallelujah! Glory, Hallelujah!" Mama Sarah shouted with joy.

Mama Sarah kissed and hugged me and Pot so tight, we could hardly breathe. She and Aunt Kate were so happy. They were so happy until they never stopped to question how all this happened and where the money came from. They never asked how the college got our names or anything. I wouldn't dare tell them, not in a million years. Jenny did it; so Pot and I are going to make the best of it. Heaven help us if anyone ever finds out how all this happened.

Later that day, I helped Mama Sarah take the ironing to Deacon Johns. Mama Sarah looked so proud when she told him her little Anna Two was going to college just like Jenny. It was like rubbing mud on his face. Jenny looked at me, winked her eye, and smiled. Jenny ran over to me, hugged me, and told me how proud she was of me. Deacon Johns just looked at me and never said a word.

I didn't know how to take this. I guess Pot didn't either. I kept asking myself if this was really real. Mama Sarah always said when God gives you something, can't nobody take it away from you. *"Please God: I hope you're behind all this. Please, let this be a blessing and not a lesson. I pray in the name of Jesus. I will never do anything bad ever again."*

This was a new beginning for all three of us. I stayed away from Jenny as much as I could for the next few weeks. Pot did the same. We didn't want to bring any attention to ourselves by being together. We didn't want anyone to wonder how all three of us ended up going to college in Nashville, Tennessee. Jenny had taken a hell of a chance, and we knew we had to play it safe.

Time passed, and everything was perfect. We were busy packing our bags. Going to college was now a reality. Mama Sarah packed so many can goods until Pot and I could have started our own food store. Aunt Kate and Big Daddy drove me and Pot. I never knew Nashville was so far away. We stopped two times for me and Pot to go to the bathroom. Not that I had to pee, but my butt was tired from sitting so long. I enjoyed the scenery though. Crossing the Tennessee River was nice. It reminded me of a bedtime story Mama Sarah once told me about Harriet Tubman singing about the Tennessee River as a signal, directing the slaves through the under ground railroad. Also, September was the month in 1787 that James Madison wrote the United States Constitution. By Mama Sarah's standards, this was a very good month. I felt good, looking out the window as we drove. College was going to be good for us. This was more than a dream come true; it was a miracle!

College was going to be a great experience for the girls. A quantum leap into success; leading to better lives for all three of them. Their imagination was at work and they were creating magnificent moments to treasure. But with all this goodness came pain, heartache, and shame. College was a great teacher and they learned more in those years than at any other time in their lives.

****

We finally arrived. Everything looked just as I expected. College students were everywhere and the campus was huge. It was a very hot and humid day and the registration lines appeared to be miles long. This was the first time I had ever seen Aunt Kate sweat. Getting us registered and settled into our dorm room was a task. At the end of that second day, I believe Aunt Kate was happy to kiss me and Pot goodbye.

The minute Aunt Kate and Big Daddy drove off the parking lot, Pot put on the shortest hot pants she could find, to scout the campus for new friends. Pot loved attention any way she could get it. Still and all, everything went well for us, and as the days passed, I thought to myself, *"I think I'm going to like it here."*

The food was good. The staff was nice and the Professors treated us like grownups. Of course, Pot was on the front row in every male Professor's class, hoping to make an easy "A" with her legs open. Pot is so crazy! She keeps me laughing all the time. I don't know what I would do without her.

Two whole months passed before we heard anything from Jenny. I'm sure Deacon Johns had everything to do with that. But I knew, sooner or later, Jenny would find her way to me and Pot.

One evening, just before dusk, several of us were sitting on the steps in front of our dorm, watching the guys walk by. And lo and behold, up drove Jenny in a brand new car. Pot and I were ecstatic! We jumped and screamed with joy. We were so happy to see Jenny. And words couldn't express how delighted we were to see Jenny so happy. Deacon Johns had finally done something nice for once in his life.

Before our first year of college was over, Jenny had taught me and Pot how to drive. We went everywhere in Nashville. Pot and I got our drivers' license and we chauffeured Jenny all over the place. We learned the city of Nashville better than we knew Memphis. The three of us were together as one. We were determined to succeed and be the best we could be. Our grades were good, and all I could feel was, *"look out life; here we come."*

Pot and I took many of our classes together. We spent many late nights studying to help each other. Some of our classes were a bit hard, but we hung in there. We were driven, and nothing was going to stop us. We were also a little popular around campus too. We can thank Jenny for that. Her picking us up in her bright, shiny new car with a Vanderbilt sticker across the rear window, made us seemed luxurious and stylish, with friends in high places.

I was so happy and we had so much fun together. Sometimes I had to remind myself to write home to Mama Sarah. And if Deacon Johns knew Jenny was riding me and Pot in her new car, he would have a heart attack. But according to the gossip from back home, he had other things to occupy his mind. The neighbors were saying, with Jenny away at school, Ms. Linda had gotten bored and went out and got herself a boyfriend. And Deacon Johns was having a time trying to catch them. So, Pot and I made a pact with Jenny; pledging never to discuss anything about our Nashville business in Memphis. All our Nashville business was to be kept to ourselves and shared with no one. And Jenny was so smart; she taught me and Pot how to be smooth operators and make everything appear perfectly normal.

When we drove home from school, Jenny would drop me and Pot at the Greyhound bus station in Memphis. We would call Aunt Kate and Big Daddy to pick us up. We would keep the bus ticket money and no one ever knew we rode home with Jenny. If Mama Sarah ever found out, she would take me out of college just for lying.

Jenny knew how to cover up everything, and as I have said before, Jenny is a genius. She would get a lot of good information from the rich kids at her school and pass it right on to us. As life moved on, college was good. We grew intellectually and each day was filled with memories I will never forget.

One Sunday afternoon, after church, we took our usual Sunday cruise through our favorite local park. Many students gathered there from colleges all across the city to mix and mingle in a safe, relaxed atmosphere. Students would sit on the lawn, cruise in nice cars, enjoying themselves, getting to know one another. As we cruised in Jenny's car that Sunday afternoon, an unusual looking sports car, very beautiful, approached us. Jenny blew her horn and gestured for the driver to pull over. He did. He parked, got out, and made his way over to where we were parked.

"Wow," Pot said. *"Who in the hell is that?"*

He was stunning, impressively attractive, and dressed like a well-to-do professional from New York City.

"Hey," Jenny said to him in a very pleasant tone.

"Hey. Y'all want to get out?" He asked.

All three of us got out of the car and went on the side where he was. Jenny immediately introduced us.

"David," Jenny said. *"This is Ann and Pot, my two best friends. Ann and Pot, this is David, my boyfriend."*

Pot and I were shocked. We both said *"Hi"* at the same time.

The sudden blow of him being Jenny's boyfriend practically made me and Pot dizzy. Her *"boyfriend"* Jenny had never mentioned a boyfriend in all her born day. I had never been so surprised. Who was this guy? Where did he come from?

We stood and talked for a short while. Most of that time, he kept his eyes on Pot. I could see Jenny was into him though. She had that glow about her that every woman has when she lands that special guy she wants to hold on to. He was about 6 feet tall, weighing about 220 lbs, fair-skinned, and inherently buff. His hair was of a coarse texture with enough waves to make a mermaid sea sick: No conk, all natural waves, waiting for a beautiful damsel to run her fingers through. But there was something about him I couldn't put my finger on. Something within my Spirit made me

93

feel a little uneasy about him. I guess it was another crazy intuition bobbing around in my head, so I chilled and didn't give it another thought. All three of us were hoping for that dream guy to be in love with forever; so, I prayed that we all would make the right choice.

****

The next few months everything was all about David. He was quite a guy with the students on his campus and the students on Jenny's campus too. His parents were rich and in this world, money can buy anything. I was surprised though, at how friendly he was with many of the Professors. They were virtually on first name basis. He was invited to their homes and occasionally went on short trips with them. Everyone was very friendly in David's circle of friends, and Jenny fitted right in with them, she came from money too. Pot and I were more or less spectators just along for the ride.

Jenny said it was good to interact with the upper echelon. She said it would help us mature and grow intellectually. I did agree with her. We were always exposed to something new: exotic foods, imported wines, million dollar homes and Pablo Picassos. Some of the homes were huge and staffed with servants. We saw lots of high class living, but I wouldn't trade it for living with Mama Sarah, a safe and comfortable little nest filled with warmth, kindness and love.

The one thing I didn't like about rubbing elbows with the elite was the drugs. Many of them felt it was okay to use drugs. Marijuana, pills, cocaine, you name it and they had it at their parties. Sometimes the parties got wild. At that point, Pot, Jenny, and I would leave early. That kind of partying wasn't our thing. I always remembered a question Mama Sarah ask a young man in our neighborhood who always followed the wrong crowd. Mama Sarah asked him: *"If your friends kiss a monkey's behind, are you going to kiss that monkey's behind too?"* Mama Sarah told him *"to always have the courage to say no."*

David respected our decisions and still included me and Pot in almost everything he and Jenny did. And he always insisted on paying for everything. I wish Pot and I had money like that. In my heart I believed someday we really would. I truly believed that someday we really would!

Chapter 7

Stepping into deeper waters

In May, 1971, David was graduating from Meharry. He wasn't leaving Nashville. His parents had arranged an Internship for him at a local hospital, which made Jenny very happy.

David's parents were coming for the graduation and Jenny was a bit nervous about meeting them. David's mother was a Gynecologist and his father owned his own ship building company and Jenny wanted to impress them.

I must say, they were the strangest Black people I had ever met. You could see right off, they didn't like Jenny. When David introduced us, disappointment was written all over their face. When he introduced Jenny as his girlfriend, his mother turned to him and scolded him as if he was a child.

"What are you getting yourself into now?" David's Mother exclaimed! *"You are not here to take on charity cases. You are here to become a doctor. You do not have time for foolishness."*

I was stunned. But Pot, Jenny, and I still respected her like we were taught to respect our elders. We didn't say a word. David insisted we join them for dinner. Not wanting to leave Jenny alone with them, Pot and I accepted his invitation.

I couldn't wait for the evening to end. If I never saw his parents again, that would have been okay with me. That lady interrogated us to no end. I believe she thought all Black girls in the South had babies, our parents picked cotton, and we still used outhouses. I thought to myself: *God please help her. She's among that group of Black people who hate their own race and see many of their people as indigent and poverty stricken beggars. They see their people as being lazy, evil, and itching to have sex. But if they examined their own consciousness, they would discover that they belittle others to make themselves look big. People like that have no honor. They are hypocrites, traitors, and very uncaring. I would always pray for them: "May God have mercy on their souls!"*

David knew his parents didn't like us, so he tried to make it up to us. He gave each of us an invitation to The Future Professionals Black Tie Soiree; an affair many future doctors and lawyers from all across the south would attend. This was a super grand affair and not only did Pot, Jenny, and I have an invitation; we had a reserved table right up front.

Jenny said this was a celebration we had to attend. She said all the future doctors were going to be there and this could be a very intriguing event for any single young woman. For two weeks, Pot and I looked high and low for something stunning to wear. We found two evening dresses at a high-in charity boutique and Pot worked on them with her dynamic alteration skills. Pot could sew anything. She learned from Mama Sarah and made all A's in Home Economics. That was her major in High School. Pot put rhinestones all around the cleavage of the purple dress she found for herself. She lowered the back down to her waist and altered the zipper down the back from the waist to the hem. The dress we found for me was a dull snake skin ivory. Pot removed the sleeves, lowered the back, altered the waist to fit my tiny waist, put a split on the side up to my thigh, and dyed the dress a very light pale pastel golden yellow. I was stunning. I looked so sexy and gorgeous in that snake skin dress; I wanted to send my snapshot to Jet Magazine. I slipped into my six inch spike heeled shoes, painted my lips red, and was ready for a night to remember.

I was rushing Pot because it was getting late and Pot had a history of always being late. Finally, Pot came to our dorm room from the shower. She looked at me and burst into laughter.

"What's so funny?" I asked.

"You," Pot said, laughing. *"Girl, you are the perfect little lady of the evening. You look at least twenty. That dress is making a power-packed statement on you."* Pot started to laugh again.

"Are you saying I look good or what?" A hurtful and embarrassed feeling came over me.

"Yes. Oh yes!" Pot said. With a fake silly grin on her face.

"Come on, Pot." I said. *"Don't play. Do I look good or what?"*

"For real Ann: You look good."

"Then why are you laughing?" I asked Pot.

"I laughed because I was shocked." Pot said. *"I've never seen you look like a big girl before. You always look like a six grader. But tonight you look like a real whore.* (Pot laughing) *A real "whore" girl: and I promise you, you will get a man tonight. If you don't, I'll give you one of mine."* (Pot laughed again).

Ann was silent. Pot was really a little jealous, but she didn't know how to handle it. She stopped her foolish laughter and tried to make amends. She went over to Ann, put her arm around Ann's shoulder, and spoke to Ann softly:

"Whores are real Ann. All those bitches that made it to the top, started out as whores: Catherine the Great, Jezebel, Queen of Sheba, Nefertiti and every other woman, in some shape, form or fashion, has been a whore. You Ann, and me, we're just whores who haven't been born yet; and tonight, we're going to shake our stuff until the morning comes. So loosen up girl and stop being so uptight!"

Pot knew Ann was hurt, but she really didn't know how to make it right. She knew Ann would never be a whore. Ann was too good for that. And if anyone tried to make her a whore, Pot would have destroyed them, or died trying.

Pot loved Ann and looked upon her as a baby sister, even though Pot was only a few weeks older. Pot felt, when they were away from home, Mama Sarah left her in charge and she would never let Mama Sarah down. Mama Sarah always praised Pot, even when Pot was disobedient. She said Pot was hard headed, didn't want to listen half of the time, and never tested the waters before jumping in. She said Pot got pleasure out of pleasing other folk instead of pleasing her own self. Mama Sarah said one of these days Pot was going to get it right and be a blessing from God for all of them.

My night was spoiled before we left the dorm. All I could do was pray so I could make it through the night. All I could hear was Pot's laughter. I felt self-conscious. I felt I looked ridiculous in my homemade dress. I felt unattractive and wanted to undress and go to bed. But, I didn't. I went because I knew if I didn't go

Pot was going to be somebody's nightcap and I didn't want that to happen to her again.

As usual, because of Pot, we arrived late. It takes Pot forever and a day to get dressed. It was raining and we had to help the taxi driver find the place. This was not my night and Pot had one more time to say something stupid to me and we would have been cat fighting all over the place.

As we drove up, the valet opened the door and assisted us inside the venue. The Ballroom was captivating. I had never seen any place so glamorous in my whole life. The first thing out of Jenny's mouth was, *"Why are 'y'all so late?"* She was a little pissed, but happy we had finally gotten there. The food, the music, and the speakers were all very good. As usual that damn Pot made a fool of herself, dancing, doing the twist and twisting all over the place. She did a floor show, moving her body as if she was Salome, the daughter of Herodias, arisen from the dead. David was grinning from ear to ear. He and his colleagues loved to see Pot roll her body until her dress rose up above those fat yellow thighs of hers. One drink too many and Pot was the life of the party.

I politely walked over and asked the band to slow it down a little, and they did. Thank God, Pot came and sat her ass down. She was soaking wet. As I sharply chastised her, I felt these eyes gazing upon me from across the room. I looked up and looked into this gentleman's alluring eyes. I felt so uncomfortable to feel so uncomfortable. I looked at him again and he smiled at me. I deliberately turned my head and ignored him. He continued standing there, sipping his drink, attentively observing the establishment. I thought to myself, *"What in the hell is he up to? Why is he looking at me with all these beautiful babes in the house tonight? I sure hope he knows I'm not a one night stand."*

After a short while, he walked over and asked me to dance. I wanted to say no, but I wanted to say yes so bad, I couldn't say no. Pot started to push me from my chair as if this was something that rarely happens to me. I guess she was tired of my bitching about her dancing like an idiot, making a fool of herself. So, I said yes, and I danced with him. He held me as if he regarded me as an elegant lady. I was very impressed. He smelled so good and gave a new meaning to tall, dark, and handsome. We danced several times and I was captivated by his charm.

We talked briefly and he said he was studying Law. I talked about my plans to graduate with a degree in Accounting. I introduced Pot and Jenny to him as my best friends. Before the night was over, he asked if he could telephone me sometimes. I told him he could, and gave him the telephone number to my dorm. His name was Matthew Middleton and I sure hoped I would see him again.

Pot and Jenny talked about Matthew as we drove back to our campus.

"Ann," Jenny said. *"Matthew is so cute, and a gentleman too. He walked you to the car and everything,"*

"Of course he walked her to the car." Pot said. *"The man is working on a Law Degree, that's his field. Like all other shysters, he knows the first step to taking a woman to bed is to walk her to her car!"*

"Shut up, Pot," Jenny said. *"You're drunk. Every man is not out to take a woman to bed."*

"That's shit!" Pot shouted. *"Show me one that's not. Even that damn, no good, David of yours, tell me he wasn't out to take your ass to bed."*

"Shut up. Both of you" I yelled! *"I just met Matthew! Surely I'm wise enough to know when a man is just some Joe Blow trying to take me to bed. Give me some credit. Let's talk about something else!"*

102

We all remained silent for the remainder of our drive. Jenny dropped me and Pot off at our dorm. It was Pot's turn to stay by the phone for Jenny's call, to say she made it safely, but Pot was too intoxicated. I helped Pot get in bed and she was asleep before I could say *"Jack Robinson."*

I thought about Matthew while I waited for Jenny's call. He was the first decent guy who had shown me attention in a very long time. I hoped he was real and true. I hope he was sent to me by God and he is everything I could ever hope for. He is so handsome and clean looking. Clean-shaven, slim build; beautiful brown eyes and skin of a ripe Georgia peach. His attire was awesome and he conducted himself as a perfect gentleman. I was very impressed.

Suddenly the phone rang. It was Jenny, acknowledging her safe arrival at her dorm. Ann bided her goodnight, went back to her room, and went to bed. Ann's sleep was calm and serene as that of a newborn princess.

Eight days passed and no telephone calls from Matthew. Every time the phone rang, Ann hoped it would be him. No call on day nine. No call on day ten.

Early the next Saturday morning, there was a loud knock on Ann and Pot's dorm room door. They were sleeping like hibernating grizzly bears. They had had a long night celebrating at a Greek festival. The festival lasted until the break of dawn. They didn't want to get up to answer the door, but the knocks got harder and harder. Knock, knock, knock; knock! Ann finally got up to answer the door.

"Who is it?" I ask.

"It's Ms. Caffey, Ann. You have a telephone call."

"Yes ma'am. I'll be there in a minute."

Ann hurried into her robe and slippers and rushed to the telephone; believing it may be Matthew Middleton. The telephone call she had wished for had finally come.

"Hello." I said.   It was Aunt Kate.

"Hey, baby."

"Aunt Kate. What's the matter? Is everything okay?"

"Yes, baby, it is. Everyone here is okay and well. I just wanted to tell you Ms. Mozella passed away this morning. I thought you may want to know."

"Oh Aunt Kate, for real, I'm so sorry. What happened?"

"I'm so sorry too, Baby. She fell out at her home. An ambulance was called but she passed before they got her to the hospital."

"I'm so sorry to hear that. How is Mama?"

"She's okay," Aunt Kate said. *"But we know it's not easy for her. Ms. Mozella was her best friend. They will probably have her home going service next Saturday. I wanted to know if you wanted to come to be with Mama, to lift her Spirit."*

"Yes ma'am. I sure do. Mama needs me now, and I need to be there for her."

"Yes, baby. I agree. I'll send you a bus ticket. Big and I will pick you up when you get here."

"Yes ma'am.   I'll call you as soon as I get the ticket and let you know what time I'll be leaving."

"Okay baby. I love you. I'll tell Mama I talked to you."

"Okay. Love you too Aunt Kate. Bye."

"Bye."

Ann was saddened by the sad news. She slowly walked back to their room. Pot was still sleeping.   Ann just laid there, on her bed, thinking how sad Mama Sarah must be to lose her best friend.   Ann told Pot everything when Pot woke up.

I got the bus ticket Aunt Kate sent and Jenny and Pot took me to the bus station. David rode with us. I didn't feel good about that because I could feel he was happy to see me leave. He went on and on about how he was going to take care of Pot and Jenny while I was gone, but I knew that was a lie. I didn't trust his ass, not one little bit. I went on to Memphis though; this was one time I knew Mama needed me.

I didn't know how Mama Sarah would take Ms. Mozella's funeral. Mama Sarah believed if you wanted to, you could live forever.   She believed all human beings were made in the image of our Father God, and that God is the God of the living. She believed Jesus gave his life for us to live, not for us to die. Mama Sarah said people die because they believe they are supposed to die. I wasn't sure what to think. There were so many unanswered questions. Questions like, why do babies die?   I really don't understand, so as for me, I'll believe as Mama Sarah believes. I want to live forever, and when Jesus comes back, I want to serve him forever in our perfect world just like Mama Sarah wants too. I'm going to eat right, exercise, love, and live. Trees live hundreds of years; so can I.

Aunt Kate and Big Daddy picked me up at the bus station in Memphis. I was happy to see them. I told Aunt Kate I didn't know what to say to Mama to make her feel better. Aunt Kate said for me to do less talking and more listening. She said that would help Mama more than anything else.

****

Mama Sarah was glad to see me. We hugged more than ever before. The funeral was short, precious, and very beautiful. It was held outside on the church ground and the weather was perfect for that occasion.

After the repast, I tried to telephone Pot and Jenny, but neither of them was available to take a telephone call. I knew David and his colleagues were having a business meeting, but I didn't think Pot and Jenny would attend. I tried hard to focus my attention on Mama Sarah's circumstances, but it was very difficult. I believed something was going on in Nashville and Pot and Jenny needed me to be there. However, I made myself focus on Mama Sarah. It was very clear she needed me, and I was there for her. Later that afternoon, many neighbors and friends gathered at Mama Sarah's house. After all the company left, Aunt Kate and I helped Mama Sarah put the food away, clean the kitchen and get the house in order. After that, Aunt Kate went to bed and Mama Sarah was lying on her bed reading the Bible.

"Mama," I said to Mama Sarah. *"Can I get you some warm peach tree leaf tea?"*

"Naw baby," Mama Sarah said. *"Come here and talk to me for a while."*

106

I got in bed beside Mama Sarah just as I did when I was a child, and I listened.

"Ann, my darling baby doll;" Mama Sarah said. *"Always expect good things to happen in your life. God loves us. He wants us to keep our minds focused on good things and be happy. Always believe and know that God is the Spirit that lives within us. Jesus was our great teacher and He taught that we are all One with our Father God. Jesus taught that death came by man, not by God. God is life! Jesus is life and we are connected to life as long as we desire to be. Believe forever Ann, and know that Life is truly everlasting, forever. Believe this and live."*

"I will miss Mozella and grieve for her. She was my dear friend. But always remember Ann, people die because they choose to, not because it's necessary. God's Word teaches that death has been abolished. It teaches that there is no more death, no more sickness, no more lack and no more pain. Those things are just illusions brought upon man by his own mind. Always choose life. Jesus said he came to this world that we may have life, not death; and, that we may have life everlasting. You understand Ann?"

"Yes ma'am." I said.

****

That same night, in Nashville, Tennessee, things got wild. Johnson White, one of David's rich friends, invited a few friends to his home to meet his business associate Atticus Sharp. Atticus was a very powerful businessman with wealth ranging in the hundreds of millions of dollars. He was in Nashville, exploring possibilities of establishing a sister Corporation there, from his major Corporation in Memphis.

Atticus Sharp's Corporation transported over 50% of all goods in the United States and he was negotiating contracts to transport goods all over the world. Johnson White was an investor and hoped his colleagues would become shareholders too. Why was David invited? That's a question I don't think anyone could answer. He didn't have a lot of money, his parents did; but, he would make one believe that all their money was really his money. David was sharp, very clever, and his ability to influence and persuade people was that of a con artist. David would not have missed this opportunity for anything in the world. He asked Johnson White if he could attend.

After a long, draining meeting, everyone was ready to relax, and have a few drinks. There was plenty of booze, good conversation, and men. A perfect time and place for David's contemptible mind to be at work.

David had asked Jenny and Pot to meet him there. Pot and Jenny were both beautiful Black women. David believed White men loved beautiful Black women and in David's mind Pot and Jenny would be a very interesting pair. David hoped somebody may want somebody to spend the night.

Pot and Jenny finally arrived and of the seven people there, they were the only women. Pot loved sexy attire to accentuate her beautiful gifts; a pleasure, pleasing to the eyes of almost every man. And Jenny, dressed in an expensive business suit, was exemplified as a smart, strong, bold business woman, all about business. Plus, Jenny was well informed and could communicate well on any level. As a matter of fact, the gentlemen there that night, were very impressed with Jenny's view points on how to develop a multi million dollar business plan. However, Jenny and Pot both were soft spoken, vulnerable, and easy; always needing Ann to save the day. But that night Ann was in Memphis, far, far away, and David knew it.

David made drinks for everyone. There was lots of laughter, soft music in the background; and, most of them drinking much too much. All eyes were on Pot as she worked the room, going from the sofa to the bar as David fixed her one drink after another.

Jenny had a couple of drinks too, but was well in control to discern that David was up to no good. Jenny wanted David to keep her around, so she didn't question anything he did. She loved him and would go along with anything to keep him.

Pot could barely stand up. She had had far too much to drink. David asked White if Pot could lay down in one of his bedrooms until she felt better. White said yes, she could.

David took Pot to one of the bedrooms and undressed her. Pot was so out of it she didn't know what was happening. He laid her on the bed, spread her legs, and placed the bed sheet over her, partially revealing her nakedness. He dimmed the lights in the bedroom and returned to the room with the guest.

Jenny was sitting at the bar, praying to God that nothing happened between Pot and David in that bedroom. Several minutes later, David asked White to look in on Pot to make sure everything was okay with her, and he did.

The moment White entered the bedroom, the sight of Pot lying on the bed naked caused him to be overcome with an uncontrollable erection. Being mildly intoxicated and emotionally at a point of weakness, his burning desire was overpowering; he had to satisfy his intense desire to make love. White closed the door, undressed, and gently snuggled himself comfortably between Pot's thighs. He entered her with ease as he held her close to him. Pot's warm, soft, moist part that holds, passionately accepted his entrance desirously. And in her intoxicated state, she could only moan and respond with passion. White stayed with her for almost an hour. Their passion flowed and their stirring arousing thrill was achieved over and over again.

When Johnson White finally came to himself, he knew what had happened was totally out of character for him. But what was done was done and he couldn't take it back. He gently removed his personal package, got out of bed, gently pulled the covers over Pot, got dressed, and returned to his guests. Johnson White hoped Pot would never remember what happened to her that night. As he returned to his guest, Jenny immediately rushed into the room where Pot was. Jenny, David and the other guests suspected what may have happened in that bedroom that night, but Pot never remembered what actually happened to her.

Jenny hurriedly helped Pot into her clothes, helped her to stand, and the two of them left Johnson White's home through a rear door and drove to the dorm. It was a struggle for Jenny to get Pot to her dorm room, but somehow she did. Jenny helped Pot into bed and safely arrived to her own dorm that night. The next morning, Pot could feel that something sexually had happened to her, but she couldn't remember exactly what, and Jenny never told her.

The following day was Sunday. That morning, Kate and Big took Ann to the Greyhound bus station to travel back to Nashville. Ann didn't really want to leave Mama Sarah, but Pot and Jenny hadn't called her, so she was anxious to get back to be assured that everything was okay. When Ann arrived at the bus station in Nashville, Pot and Jenny were there waiting for her.

As soon as I got off the bus I knew something had gone wrong. I could see it in Pot and Jenny's eyes. They were hiding something. They both lied and pretended everything went well while I was gone, but I didn't believe them. I could feel they were lying, but I was so happy to be back, I just decided to accept their lies.

We got my things packed in Jenny's car and were on our way to the dorm. Mama Sarah had packed a big box for us: pound cake, sweet potato pie, canned peaches and everything. I was so happy to be back with my two best friends.

We had a good time that evening going through the box I brought back from Memphis. Jenny finally left and Pot had eaten so much pound cake until she was full and sleepy. Pot rolled her hair and went to bed. I wasn't sleepy at all; so, I got ready for bed, relaxed, and started to read a book. Suddenly there was a knock at the door. *Knock, knock.*

"Yes?" I answered

"Ann, it's me Ms. Caffey. There's a telephone call for you."

"Yes ma'am. Here I come."

I hurried to the telephone. I was so scared. I had just left home. What has happened, this quick? I hoped nothing had happened to Mama.

"Hello," I said to the party holding.

"Hello. My, you're a hard person to catch up with," he quipped.

"Oh Hi," I said. *"It's Matthew, right?"*

"Yes." Matthew said. *"Thanks for remembering."*

Ann was so happy Matthew called. She couldn't have desired anything any sweeter. Their conversation went on and on. It was a late Sunday evening and many of the girls on Ann's dorm floor had retired for the evening. Therefore, Ann and Matthew could talk as long as they wanted. The conversation was so good for Ann. She needed to feel good and laugh; and that's just what she did.

"The first couple of times I called and asked for you," Matthew said, *"the party didn't know who I was talking about. I guess they thought I was calling for a White girl. Who gave you that White girl's name anyway?"*

"What? You are so crazy." I said. *"I do not have a White girl's name."*

"Sarah Anna! Come on now." Matthew said. *"That's a White girl's name if I've ever heard one."*

"Well, as you have seen, I am not a White girl." I laughed.

"Hold up now." Matthew said. *"Don't be offended. I like White girls, especially the chocolate ones!"*

Ann and Matthew both laughed out loud. Their conversation went on and on that night. Matthew Middleton was indeed a perfect gentleman. He was the youngest of three siblings, raised with southern hospitality, and the third generation of attorneys. He was charismatically endowed with much wisdom and very competent in many areas of the law. He was taught by his parents to be fair, decent and have a high value of honor and respect for God. He was funny, loveable, and kind, and Ann looked forward to talking to him again and again and again.

Chapter 8

Facing unbelievable events

As the weeks passed, I clearly discerned that something happened between Pot and Jenny while I was in Memphis. Things were a bit strange between the two of them. They were not talking to each other as much and they didn't seem to be close like they used to be. I just couldn't figure it out. My mind was so occupied with Matthew until he was all I wanted to think about. But in the back of my mind, I kept feeling something went wrong while I was in Memphis.

Matthew and I had been seeing each other about six weeks and most of our spare time was spent together. Our kisses were long and serious and he was beginning to hold me closer and closer each time we kissed. I didn't know what to do. I was afraid to think what could happen next. I wanted him and I believed he wanted me just as much, and each time we were together, I became more and more afraid. I didn't want him to know I was still a virgin. I was embarrassed and ashamed. I needed to talk this out with Pot and Jenny.

Ann told Pot and Jenny she needed to talk to them. She said it was concerning something very serious and they needed to meet right away. Later the next day, the three of them got together in Ann and Pot's dorm room. Ann explained that she

113

was very tense and uneasy about what may happen if Matthew found out she was still a virgin. Ann told them she and Matthew were becoming very close and she didn't know how to handle a situation like that.

"Just tell him Ann." Pot said. *"If he cares about you, it shouldn't matter whether you're a virgin or not. He should be happy to know he's your first, and you haven't been sleeping around."*

"But what if it does matter?" Jenny added. *"He may feel she's too inexperienced and immature. He may feel that being her first may cause her to be too attached and he doesn't need that. Just getting out of Law School and trying to pass the Bar. He will not want to deal with the drama of some immature school girl, who just lost her virginity, trying to hang on to him."*

"Jenny," Pot said. *"We're not talking about some Negro like David. Matthew is a real man; a man who's loving and kind and very understanding. He's nothing like that con man you're trying, hard as hell, to hang on too."*

"You see, Pot! There you go," Jenny yelled! *"You're always bad mouthing David! David is a good man. I don't know why you hate him so!"*

"Okay, okay," I said. *"I didn't want this to turn into a shouting match. I came to y'all because y'all are all I've got! I need to know what to do!"*

"Damn," Pot shouted! *"Just give the Nigger some Ann, and shut the fuck up! If he likes it, it won't matter if it's a virgin cat or a cat that's been passed around. Believe me, he will be back for more!"*

The paw-wow ended inconclusively, with the girls going to the dairy bar for a banana split. Ann did tell Matthew she was a virgin, which he suspected all along. He told her he was elated to know that and that nothing would ever happen until she was sure she was ready.

As time passed, Ann and Matthew grew even closer, but so far nothing had happened sexually. They spent most of their time developing a special friendship, building trust and confidence in each other. They talked, went to the movies and ate from the same popcorn. They took long walks in the park and frequently had lunch and dinner together. Ann was spending more time with Matthew than she was with Pot and Jenny. Many nights, when Matthew dropped Ann off at her dorm, Pot was already in bed and asleep.

Things would soon change though. The semester was ending and Matthew was leaving for a six month internship at one of the most prestigious Law Firms in Washington, D. C. Ann was sad about him leaving, but it really was a blessing. Graduation was getting close and she needed this time to pour all her energy into studying and planning for "what's next" after graduating college. Ann was falling in love with Matthew, but she needed this time to concentrate on her own life. Jenny was secure with Medical School and Ann didn't want to be a college grad with no direction. Ann needed this time away from Matthew to study and plan.

****

Matthew's big day finally came and he was off to experience what it's like to be an attorney in the real world. Ann rode with him to the airport. They said their goodbyes and Ann brought his car back to a long-term parking facility near his apartment. Jenny picked Ann up from the parking facility to take her back to her dorm. Ann was very quiet.

"You okay?" Jenny asked.

"Sure, I'm okay. But Jenny, I believe I'm really in love with Matthew. I can feel his Spirit. I can't explain it. But this is more than a connection, or a courtship. I believe I truly do love him."

Jenny chuckled, saying. *"As much as you love Mama Sarah's sour cream pound cake, and sweet potato pie?"* They both laughed. Then Jenny went on to say: *"Well, if you can say yes to that, then girl, you're really in love. That's what my stomach wants to love on right about now. In two weeks it will be Thanksgiving Ann, Thanksgiving!"*

****

Time passed and the girls were all packed up in Jenny's car to go home for the Thanksgiving weekend. Ann and Jenny sat up front and chattered all the way to Memphis, while Pot curled up on the back seat and slept. Ann and Jenny talked about everything from putting on make-up to planning a wedding. Before they knew it, they were at the Greyhound bus station in Memphis. Ann and Pot waited patiently for Kate and Big to pick them up, looking forward to a wonderful weekend.

Thanksgiving was great and they had lots of fun. Mama Sarah cooked the perfect Thanksgiving dinner and everyone had a great time. Amy Mae, Charlie Murphy, and the boys came down from Detroit, making the Thanksgiving Holiday a feast to remember.

The following Sunday morning, all goodbyes were said and everyone headed back home. Ann and Pot took a taxi to the

bus station. Jenny picked them up and they zipped down the highway back to Nashville. Everyone was stuffed from all that eating and was looking forward to another great feast on Christmas.

This was the girls' last year in college. After Christmas, one more semester and all three of them would be done with their first college degree. This would be a major accomplishment and all three of them were studying hard to make it a reality.

****

Wow, the last day of finals, and one more test to take. Pot and I are both winners. We did well on our other exams. I know we're going to ace Professor Hendrix's exam. Graduation here we come! I thank God for this point in our lives. And I'm so grateful our families and friends are ready to celebrate our victory.

Ann could hardly wait to walk into Professor Hendrix's class and see the smile on Pot's face. Despite all their adversities and sleepless nights, they had almost made it and graduation was only one semester away.

Ann entered Professor Hendrix's class energetically, knowing her and Pot's last exam was about to be behind them. As Ann entered the classroom, she was stunned; Pot was not in class. Five minutes passed, then ten. Ann was getting worried. Professor Hendrix began to pass out the test booklets. He stopped at Ann's desk.

"Where's Miss Love?" he asked.

117

"She's on her way Sir. Can we give her a couple more minutes please?" Professor Hendrix nodded his head yes. He had already stalled five minutes. He couldn't wait much longer. I gathered my belongings and went to his desk.

"Professor Hendrix," I said. *"I have to go find her. She was on her way. Something must have happened. Please excuse me, so I can check on her."*

I believe Professor Hendrix thought Pot was messing off. He didn't say anything. He continued looking through the papers in his hand. I took it upon myself to read his expression as him saying yes. I hurried out of the classroom wondering to myself:

"Where in the hell can Pot be? That damn Pot worries the hell out of me at times. Her ass better be dead, I do know that, and if she isn't, I'm going to kill her ass today. She knows we need this class to graduate. This exam is one third of our grade. Damn, Pot. Where in the hell are you?"

Ann looked everywhere for Pot. She looked in the library; the student center and the cafeteria. She couldn't find Pot anywhere. Ann continued looking for Pot as she mumbled to herself.

"I know this heifer can't still have her ass in the bed."

Ann headed for the dorm, furious. She ran up the stairs and hastily opened their dorm room door and Pot was there, lying on the floor. Blood was everywhere. Ann was shocked and speechless after seeing Pot in that condition. She saw a long, sharp object in Pot's hand and thought Pot had stabbed

herself. Ann thought Pot was dead! She didn't know what to do. She fell to her knees and covered her mouth with her hands; too fearful to let a sound come out of her mouth. All Ann could do was bow to the floor and sob silently, knowing in her heart, she had to do something and fast. She started to mumble to herself in a whisper of a voice.

"Oh Pot, what did you do? What did you do Pot? What did you do? Oh my God, I've got to call Jenny."

Ann, sobbing and tearing, helplessly pulled a sheet from her bed, and covered Pot from her chest down, to cover the tremendous amount of blood on the floor. The blood softly seeped through, soaking the sheet as if the sheet wasn't there.

Tearful and frightened, trying not to panic, Ann left the room, locked the door and ran to the phone to call Jenny. No answer. Ann hung up the telephone and set out to find Jenny.

Ann had never been on Vanderbilt's campus. All she could remember is what Jenny had told her. Ann hurriedly ran down the stairs, out to the street, running as fast as she could to find Jenny. Suddenly, a taxi cab drove beside her. The taxi driver was wondering "where in the world is this crazy girl running too." Ann saw him and flagged him down. He stopped.

"Mr.," I said. *"I need to get to Vanderbilt's campus right now. Please take me."*

"What do you want at Vanderbilt's campus girl?" He asked.

"I've got to get there right now, please Sir. Something terrible has happened!"

119

"You ain't going to get me in trouble are you?"

"No Sir. Please! I've got to get there fast!"

"Come on." The taxi driver said. *"Get in, I'll take ya."* The driver took off, driving to Vanderbilt's campus with Ann in his cab.

"Why are you running and crying like a fool for?" He asked.

"I'm okay, Sir. I'll be all right." I wiped away my tears with my arm and wrist.

The taxi driver, who was well familiar with Vanderbilt's campus, took Ann immediately to the building she described. Ann jumped out of the taxi, running to the Pathology building, as fast as she could. The taxi driver immediately drove away, hoping no one saw Ann get out of his taxi.

As Ann rushed to find Jenny, many students looked shocked to see this strange Black girl on campus sobbing and crying, running in fear.

The buildings on Vanderbilt's campus looked exactly as Jenny had described them. Ann ran to the third floor of the Pathology building and peered through the glass in each door until she saw Jenny, in class, sitting at a desk. Ann opened the door to the classroom and ran straight to Jenny, sobbing and trembling with fear.

Jenny was embarrassed and shocked by the state of Ann's condition. The class professor and the students were speechless; words could not express what they had suddenly seen. This Black girl, on her knees, sobbing, telling Jenny she must come quick!

Jenny helped Ann to her feet; gathered her books and quickly left the room.   In the hallway, Jenny stopped for a quick second to try to shake some sense into Ann.

"Ann, calm down, calm down! Tell me what's wrong!"

"Jenny," I said.   *"I believe Pot is dead!"*

"Pot is dead!"   Jenny shouted!   *"What do you mean she's dead?"*

"She didn't come to class.   I went to look for her and found her in   our dorm room, lying on the floor and blood was everywhere!"

Jenny picked up her books from the floor and started to run to her car. Ann was running beside her. They got into Jenny's car and headed for Pot and Ann's dorm.

"I was scared Jenny."   I said.   *"I didn't know what to do.   I was so scared! I believe Pot's dead."*

"What happened?"   Jenny shouted.   *"Did she cut herself or did she fall and hurt herself on something in the room?"*

"I don't know!" I said.   *"I don't know what happened! I don't know!"*

Jenny was shouting and driving as fast as she could. Ann was crying and sounding like a confused child. Upon their arrival, they both hurried out of the car and ran to the dorm room. Pot was still laying there, on the floor, blood on her hands and on her clothes; she was laying in blood. The sight of Pot and all that blood was frightening to Jenny, but she kept calm. Jenny moved swiftly to examine Pot, Ann stood near frightened and scared.

"She's not dead," Jenny said softly. *"She's still breathing, but she has lost a lot of blood. We've got to get her to the hospital right now."*

Jenny tried to move Pot, just a little, to try to see where she was bleeding from. Jenny discovered a fetus amidst all the blood.

"Oh my God" Jenny exclaimed. *"It's a fetus."*

"What!" I remarked, trembling.

"A fetus," Jenny said. *"Evidently Pot was pregnant and tried to give herself an abortion. She could have killed herself!"*

"Oh my God," I shouted as I covered my mouth with my hands. *"You want me to call an ambulance?"*

"No." Jenny said. *"We can't call an ambulance. Self-induced abortions are illegal in the United States. This is a homicide. Pot could go to jail. We have to take her to the hospital ourselves. She's passed out. She has lost a lot of blood, and she's probably in pain. She's going to be okay though,"* Jenny continued to examine Pot to make sure it was okay to move her.

"What do you want me to do?" I asked Jenny.

"Get these bloody clothes off her" Jenny said. *"And put her robe on. We'll wrap her in a blanket and take her to the car.*

I'm going to call David. He's covering ER at General this week. We'll have to take her there."

Jenny was on the phone trying to reach David while Ann was nervously putting things together to transport Pot to the E.R. David answered Jenny call.

"David, thank God you're there," Jenny said to him.

"Hey Babe, what's wrong"? David asked.

"It's Pot. I have to bring her to the hospital right away. She tried to give herself an abortion."

"What!" David was startled by the news.

"Yes," Jenny said. *"The long knitting needle she used as an abortifacient device was still in her hand. She's passed out, but her breathing is good and steady. I put pressure on her abdomen several times. I believe everything aborted. Looks like the fetus membrane and placenta all expelled from the womb. Oh David it's horrible, she could have killed herself."* Jenny sounded as if she wanted to cry.

"Damn Babe!" David exclaimed. *"But listen, Honey. Get her here as fast as you can. You must bring everything with you; her bloody clothes; the fetus, the placenta, everything!"*

"Why?" Jenny asked. *"Will you have to file a police report?"*

"No!" David said. *"But you must bring all those things with you; everything! I'll be waiting for you at the staff's entry in the rear of the building; hurry!"*

Jenny did just as David instructed her. She and Ann cleaned much of the blood from Pot as fast as they could. They put a robe on Pot and wrapped her in a blanket. They placed her on a chair, locked the dorm room door, and dragged the chair to the car via the freight elevator. Pot was very weak and lethargic. Her pain was extremely severe. Her eyes were closed, and tears were running down her face.

When they reached the hospital, David was waiting for them just as he said. He and two of his staff members transferred Pot to a gurney and hastily rushed her in for treatment. David took the bag containing the fetus and other items into the hospital with him. Ann and Jenny waited in the ER waiting room. After about three hours, David came in to inform them of Pot's condition.

"She's going to be okay," David said. *"She's in recovery and doing fine."*

"Thank God," Jenny said. *"Can we take her home, or will she have to stay overnight?"*

"No," David said. *"She'll have to be admitted and stay a few days. We had to perform a total hysterectomy. The uterus was damaged, and there was nothing we could do."*

"Nothing you could do!" Jenny shouted. *"Damn, David, an idiot would have known to do a dilation and curettage and give the uterus time to heal before performing a complete hysterectomy! Whose decision was that? Someone used very poor judgment in this matter. I want to see the got-damn medical report!"*

Things were about to explode. Jenny was using profanity and getting loud. She was very upset with David for performing a

complete hysterectomy on Pot. Things were about to get out of hand, so Ann intervened to try to calm things down.

"Wait a minute y'all." I said. *"Let's calm down. We have to think about Pot. We can't fight now. Pot needs us. David, when can we see her?"* I asked.

"She'll be in recovery for another hour," David said. *"And then she'll be transferred to a room."*

"What about a police report?" Jenny inquired in a naughty tone.

"We took care of that." David said. *"She shouldn't have any problems."*

"Thanks." Jenny said; looking at David as if she wanted to wring his neck.

David left the room to return to his duties. And most of all, Jenny and Ann were happy to know Pot was okay. Jenny had to leave, but Ann stayed in the waiting room until Pot was transferred to a regular patient room.

Finally, a nurse came in and informed Ann that Pot had been transferred to a room. Ann hurried to Pot, excited and happy, knowing Pot was okay. The moment Pot saw Ann she put her hands over her face and burst into tears. Ann rushed to Pot and put her arms around her.

"It's okay. It's okay." I said to Pot, to console her. *"Don't cry Pot. It's okay."*

"Ann… Oh Ann," Pot said as she wept in despair. *"I should have told you, but I was so scared. I didn't know what to do. I just wanted everything to disappear."*

"I know, but its okay." I said. *"Everything is behind us and you're okay."*

"I don't know who I had been with." Pot said as she cried. *"I hadn't been with anyone for weeks before the Professional Ball. It's like my mind is trying to make me remember, but I can't remember a thing. It's like a dream or something. I can't remember Ann. I don't know who the father was."*

"Don't worry about it." I said. *"It's all behind us now and you're okay. And that's all that matters."*

"But, Ann," Pot said. *"I committed murder! Please forgive me! I'm so sorry. If I could take it all back, I would. I would keep my baby. I don't care who the father was, I would keep my baby, Ann. I would keep my baby."* Pot cried out loud in a painful cry.

"Its okay Pot." I said as tears ran down my face. *"It's got to be okay! Please don't cry!"* I held Pot and dried Pot's tears.

After a short while, a nurse came in and injected a sedative in Pot's IV to quiet her and help her rest. After a few minutes Pot was asleep and resting peacefully. Jenny returned and she and Ann discussed quietly how they could help Pot get through this crisis.

"How can we tell her she won't be able to get pregnant again?" Jenny asked me.

"I don't know." I said. *"How do you tell somebody something like that?"*

126

"Her surgery couldn't be helped." I said. *"It had to be done to save her life. We've got to find a way to make her understand that it had to be done."*

"I believe she'll understand." I said. *"She's got to understand. We couldn't let her die."*

Jenny and Ann pondered seriously over how they could break this horrible news to Pot. They hated to cause her anymore pain. They decided to say they would have hysterectomies too, so Pot wouldn't feel alone in this situation.

When Pot woke up, Ann and Jenny sat beside her on each side of her bed with their arms around her. They told Pot everything that had happened and what they had decided to do about it. Although Pot was sad about not being able to have another child, she couldn't believe what Jenny and Ann had decided to do.

"Are y'all crazy?" Pot shouted. *"Y'all can't do anything crazy like that. We need some babies in this family. We need somebody we can tell all this crazy stuff too."* Pot smiled although she was filled with hurt and pain.

Now that Pot was out of danger and on the road to recovery, all three of them held each other tightly and were comforted.

This mystifying episode of Ann, Pot, and Jenny's life had come and gone. They all wanted to forget what had happened and move forward, hoping it would go away and never enter their minds again.

****

Pot stayed in the hospital several days. I talked with Professor Hendrix, and explained that Pot had a severe case of food poisoning and was in the hospital. He graciously rescheduled our final exam with kindness.

Those days in the hospital with Pot were fun. I stayed with her every night and Jenny was there most of the day. Pot was afraid of hospitals and probably would have panicked if we had left her there alone. We watched television, played games, and I had my share of Pot's good hospital food. It was much better than the food in the cafeteria on campus.

The day of Pot's discharge, Jenny got there early. Pot was so ready to go home. I had cleaned our dorm room and had everything fresh and clean for her homecoming. I did everything I could to erase every thought of what had happened there. Jenny and I got Pot all packed up and waited for the nurse to discharge her.

A knock came upon the door. We all said, *"Come in"* at the same time. The door opened and two men came in carrying the longest vases of beautiful red roses we had ever seen. A third man entered the room carrying a huge basket of exotic fruit: passion fruit, mangos, little pineapples, pomegranates, exotic grapes and everything. We were stunned. We checked the cards to make sure they were in the right room. All three cards were addressed to Potianna Love, extending "Get Well" wishes. Pot signed the receipt and the delivery men were on their way. We were amazed.

During our drive to the dorm, we all tried to guess who sent the roses and fruit, but neither of us could come up with anyone.

"Pot," I said. *"Do you think it was that guy who wanted to kiss your toes at the Greek Show last month?"*

"Girl, naw, that Negro ain't got no money."

128

"Maybe it was that janitor," Jenny said, *"who's always fixing things for y'all."*

Pot smiled, as she said; *"Now you know that man has never seen a pomegranate or a mango."*

We all laughed so hard. By the time we got to the dorm, my stomach was sore from laughing. I was so happy to hear Pot laughing. My Spirit told me it wasn't going to be so difficult for her to move on after all. I was so thankful.

I got Pot all settled in; we took Professor Hendrix's exam and passed. Things were back to normal again. I was so glad it was almost Christmas. I needed so much to lay my head on Mama Sarah's shoulder and get a moment of peaceful rest. I was so glad it was almost time to go home.

Chapter 9

More than just friends

Two days before Christmas Eve, Jenny and Ann were ready to go home for the Holidays. Pot was staying in Nashville. She was determined to find the mystery guy who sent her the roses and fruit when she was in the hospital.

Jenny and Ann wished her well and were on their way. Mama Sarah and Kate would be away, helping Mrs. Payne bring her husband home from the hospital, so Jenny was going to drop Ann off at home.

Jenny and I were so glad to be going home. We were both day dreaming about Mama Sarah's mustard greens and hot water cornbread. As for Pot, since she was all into finding her mystery guy, I wasn't going to bring her any food back from Memphis. No pound cake, no homemade rolls, no nothing!

Our ride home was pleasant. The sun was beaming down and Jenny and I rode with the windows down. The wind was blowing, and the cool air was like a massage to my head and face. I was about to doze off to sleep when Jenny asked a question I thought would have never come out of her mouth. Jenny shocked the dickens out of me. But there was too much sorrow in my Soul to tell her the things I heard Mama Sarah and Ms. Mozella talk about when I was a child. It would break Jenny's heart. When she looked into my eyes, I'm sure she knew I was lying. She knew that I knew something that I couldn't tell. I wanted to tell her; but I couldn't.

"Ann?" Jenny said very softly.

"What?" I said. I had my head laid back and my eyes closed. I opened my eyes and slightly raised my head to hear what Jenny was about to say. Then, this question came out of her mouth.

"Have you ever heard Mama Sarah mention anything about my real mom and dad?"

Ann was silent for a moment. She didn't know what to say or how to answer that question.

"Your real mom and dad: No, I've never heard Mama Sarah say anything about anybody but Deacon Johns and Ms. Valerie. Why you ask me a crazy question like that?"

"I don't know." Jenny said. *"I guess I'm trying to find a way to get me a crazy check."*

We both laughed. *"Girl, you are so crazy."* I said. *"This is how you get a crazy check."* (I crossed my eyes and stuck a straw in my nose instead of in my mouth).

Ann and Jenny both laughed and started joking about what you have to do crazy, to get a crazy check. They continued the drive and laughed most of the way home. Ann knew in her heart that Jenny was very serious, but that was a question Ann had no idea how to answer. Ann had heard the whole story

about Jenny's real parents. But Ann didn't have the faintest idea of how to put that type of pain into words. Those were words Ann didn't know how to speak.

When we arrived home, everything was quiet in the neighborhood. I guess everybody was out doing last minute Christmas shopping. Jenny helped me carry my bags in the house and suggested that I go home with her to help her with her bags. I said yes. Jenny said Deacon Johns and Ms. Linda were in Arkansas and were not expected back for hours.

I helped Jenny with her bags and before we knew it, we were talking and looking at all the beautiful paintings and art work in their home. Jenny started showing me all the clothes and shoes in her closet she had never worn. She even talked me into sitting down for a few minutes, for oatmeal cookies and a glass of homemade Hawaiian punch. We were having a great time.

Suddenly, we heard a car drive up. Jenny and I peeped through the curtains. It was Deacon Johns. He was hurrying into the house as if he was coming to put out a fire. Jenny hid me in her closet.

Deacon Johns stormed into Jenny's room like a maniac. I peered at them through a narrow opening in her closet door. He charged at Jenny like an insane madman. I could see the devil in hell in his eyes. He grabbed Jenny by her hair and slammed her against the wall. I couldn't believe the words that came out of his mouth.

"You ungrateful Bitch, Deacon Johns shouted, *what in the hell is wrong with your ass, got-damn-it? I got a call from your school today. They said you had some Nigger on campus, acting a fool in front of everybody. You crazy Bitch! What in the hell is wrong with you! I pulled all kinds of strings to get your ass in that damn school, and you're going to bring some Black Nigger on campus? Are you crazy?"*

133

"But, Daddy," Jenny said, trying to calm him. *"It wasn't like that at all. I was only trying to help my friends."*

"Your friends," he screamed, *"How in the hell can trash like that be your friends? People like that are only good for emptying your shit pot and taking out your damn trash! If I ever hear of you having a Nigger on that damn campus again, I'll...."*

Before Deacon Johns could finish, Jenny started shouting back at him.

"You don't know the half of it, Daddy! The people at that school don't care about me! They won't even sit with me at lunch or sit next to me in the classrooms! They know I'm not White, Daddy! I'm not White! I'm a Nigger Daddy! I'm a Nigger too!"

Before Jenny could continue, Deacon Johns swiftly whirled and hit Jenny in the middle of her face with his fist. She fell to the floor. Blood splattered on the wall from her nose and lip. Tears streamed down her face. Deacon Johns was furious.

"You may not be White, you ungrateful Bitch, but your ass better act like you're White! As long as I'm sticking my neck out for you, you better eat, sleep and shit White! Black folk can't help you! How do you think I got where I am? When you get back to that school, you better learn everything you can from those White folk. If they ask you to bow down and kiss their feet, you better bow your ass down and kiss their damn feet. You hear me? You bow your ass down! You ungrateful Bitch!

Deacon Johns immediately walked out of Jenny's room, slammed the front door, got in his car, and drove away. Ann was standing in the closet peeping out at Jenny lying on the floor. When Ann heard Deacon Johns' car drive away, she came out of the closet to comfort Jenny. Jenny was crying, shaking and bleeding.

"Oh Jenny, I'm so sorry." I helped Jenny to her feet. *"I'm so sorry. I'm so sorry, Jenny."*

Ann helped Jenny to the bathroom and helped her wash the blood from her face with a warm wet towel.

"It's bad to say this Ann," Jenny said. *"But I hate my own daddy."*

"Oh Jenny, please don't say that. Let's just pray and ask God to have mercy on all of us."

"Thanks Ann. I will, but we've got to get you out of here before he comes back."

Jenny let Ann out through the back door. Ann climbed over the back fence and ran home through the Back Alley way.

A couple of hours later, Mama Sarah and Kate came home. They were so happy to see Ann. Mama Sarah's cakes and pies smelled throughout the whole house. Although Ann was very sad inside, she tried to appear happy. But when it was all said and done, this was the worse Christmas Ann had ever had.

This was the worse Christmas I have ever had. Matthew snowed-in in Washington, D.C. and can't get a plane out. Pot in Nashville searching for her secret admirer; and Jenny at home with a potato on her face, too ashamed to come outside and refusing to take my telephone calls. My goodness, what did I do to bring all this misery to myself? I spent my whole Christmas break scratching Mama Sarah's head and eating sweet potato pie.

****

After the Holidays, Ann couldn't wait for the taxi cab to take her to the bus station. When the taxi arrived, she let out a long sigh of relief as if she had been home for months instead of weeks. When the taxi dropped her off at the bus station, Jenny was there waiting for her. Ann put her bags in the trunk of Jenny's car and hopped inside the car as fast as she could.

"Oh Jenny," I said; *"Am I glad to see you! Why haven't you called me? I have been on pins all during Christmas and New Year, wondering what was going on with you."*

Jenny looked at Ann with sad eyes, but she tried to appear happy.

"I needed some time to think." Jenny said. *"I've got to make some changes in my life. Life just isn't working right for me."* Jenny cranked up the car and started the drive to Nashville.

"Jenny, believe me," I said, *"things are going to get better. All three of us will soon be graduating. We can get a job, get an apartment and you can get the hell away from Deacon Johns."*

"Ann, you always know the right words to say to make things better." (Jenny reached over and put her hand over Ann's hand.) *"I want to thank you Ann, for always being so good, and always being there for me, and being there for Pot too. You and Pot are closer to me than anyone in this whole world. I thank God for you Ann."*

"I love y'all." I said. (Tears were forming in Ann's eyes.) *"You and Pot are my family. You can always count on me to be there for y'all. And I know I can count on you and Pot. The three of us are one and we're all in this thing together."*

Ann and Jenny felt a lot better, after their little talk, and had a pleasant drive to Nashville. When they arrived, Jenny dropped Ann off at her dorm and headed straight to David's place. She and David had talked over the telephone and he was eagerly waiting to see her.

Pot was nowhere to be found and none of the girls in the dorm had seen her. The room was a mess, so Ann put her things away, got their room in order and went to bed. Around ten o'clock that night, Pot came through the door.

"Where in the hell have you been?" I shouted at Pot.

"Well, Merry Christmas and Happy New Year to you, too, my darling sister." Pot said, laughing.

"It's not funny." I said. *"This was the worse Christmas I have ever had! You and Jenny both left me by myself and I didn't have any fun at all. Matthew had his ass snowed in, in Washington, D.C. and I hardly heard from him either. I'm mad!"*

Pot was still laughing. *"Well, cheer up, baby doll because I have some news that's going to knock your socks off."*

"What?" I said, as I sat up in bed eager to hear what Pot had to say!

"I found him, Ann. I found him!"

"Pot you lying girl! You mean you really found him?"

"I found him, Ann. I really found him!"

Ann and Pot both were filled with joy. They sat on the bed and Pot told Ann all about her wonderful mystery guy.

"Ann, he's so nice. We did everything together during the Holidays. He took me to places I didn't even know existed in this city. We spent three nights in this Grand Hotel and he didn't even try to have sex with me. He said we will have plenty of times in our lives later for that. He took me shopping and to First National Bank and opened a checking account for me in my own name!"

"Oh Pot; for real!" I was ecstatic.

"Oh Ann; it's almost unbelievable. He wants me to take this course next semester to get my Real Estate License. He's going to get one of his friends in Memphis to give me a job as a Real Estate Agent. I've never had anyone to care about me like that. He wants me to succeed in life and be somebody."

"Who is this man Pot, and how does he know you?"

"He's a businessman from Memphis and he owns airplanes and everything. He's very successful; I believe he's a millionaire. But Ann, listen to me, please! I don't want anyone to know about him, okay. He's a very private person and I want to keep it like that."

138

"Why?" I asked. *"Is there something wrong with him?"*

"No, but, Ann, he's a White man."

"A White man; Pot are you crazy? You can't trust a White man like that. He could be a maniac or anything."

"No, Ann. He's nothing like that at all. He's nice and kind. He's funny and he keeps me laughing all the time. He's very nice. I can't wait for him to get between my luscious thighs and pleasure me with his divine love!" Pot started to laugh.

"Girl, you are so crazy." I said. *"You just make sure you get your butt to class everyday so you can walk across that stage in May to get your Degree."* (Ann got in bed and pulled the covers up).

"I am girl." Pot said. *"But Ann, seriously, I don't want anyone to know about him at all. Not even Jenny right now."*

"Why does this have to be such a big secret?" I ask. *"I think you should find out everything about this guy before you get involved. Play it safe. Check him out. And Jenny and I need to know everything about him too."*

Speaking very softly, Pot said: *"Ann, it's Atticus Sharp."*

"Atticus Sharp! Oh Pot; for real: The Atticus Sharp?" I sat straight up in bed. I was shocked.

"Yes Ann:" Pot said; *"The Atticus Sharp."*

"Damn, Pot. But, he's a grown man, ten or fifteen years past your age."

"I know Ann, but I really want to see him! And if you ever tell anyone, I swear to you Ann, I'll kill myself! Swear to me that

you will never tell anyone and swear you will never let his name come out of your mouth! Swear to me, Ann! Swear to me!" Pot shouted!

"Okay! Okay! I swear." I said.

"And swear you will never judge me for being with him!"

"I swear Pot. Believe me, I swear. And I don't judge people! I love everyone and everything our Father God has made! Love is what I am and I love everybody. Now let's get some sleep. We have a long day ahead of us tomorrow."

Ann prayed that Pot knew what she was getting into. Ann asked God to send His angels and our ancestors to watch over Pot. Ann didn't judge Pot and she never betrayed Pot's trust.

****

The next few months were almost perfect. Spring was like a new beginning and you could feel the flavor of love all in the air. The girls were really growing up. They were diligently trying to secure gainful employment after graduation while learning about love all at the same time. Ann talked to Matthew over the telephone almost every day.

Matthew will be coming for the graduation. He said he would be here no matter what. Our conversations are getting serious. We talk on the phone as if we are cuddling in each other's arms. We haven't reached the point of saying I love you yet, but I feel it in my Spirit every time he say, *"I'm really missing you."*

The last time we were together, our kisses were long and so good. Our kisses were almost like making love. Our bodies were so close; you could feel the warmth through our clothes. I believe he wants to make love to me, and I believe I'm ready, but I'm still a little scared. *"Oh God, what am I to do? Please help me?"*

Jenny has been clinging to David every since that episode between her and Deacon Johns. And Pot study every day and night for her real estate class, with not one minute to spare to talk. I couldn't talk to Mama Sarah about my feelings for Matthew. I prayed; *"It's just you and me God; just you and me. Please don't let me make the wrong decision."*

Time passed and it was time for the girls to graduate College. Pot, Ann and Jenny were all excited about their great day. Everything had turned out right and on May 26, 1973, once again, all three of them proudly marched to Pomp and Circumstance. And I do believe Atticus Sharp was somewhere in that crowd.

The commencement exercise was awesome. Everybody was screaming and clapping for everybody. Pot and I looked so good walking across that stage to get our Bachelor Degree. That was one of the best days of my life.

I was so happy for my family to meet Matthew. He looked so good. He had on the perfect suit to look the part of an up and coming powerful attorney. My mom, dad, brothers, Aunt Kate, and even Mama Sarah, appeared to be pleased with him.

Pot's eyes and my eyes were constantly communicating and Pot's eyes gave me her approval every time. I wish Pot's sweetheart could have been there. I know they would have approved of him too. He keeps Pot so happy. She's always glowing. Her skin looks fresh and she's always laughing. And happiness was written all over Ms. Polly Mae's face. She was so proud of her baby girl. And Mr. Lowell was proud too. "Thank you God, for loving us so much."

I talked to Jenny earlier over the telephone. She was all hyped up too. She said Deacon Johns and Ms. Linda were there and David was right by her side. She said several people from home had come too. Jenny was just as happy as Pot and I was. She said her only wish was that her mother, Ms. Valerie, could be there.

Mama Sarah said May 26, is a good day: the birthday of John Wayne and Laurance S. Rockefeller. The day Lewis and Clark took their first look at the Rocky Mountains and the day of the grand opening of the Golden Gate Bridge. I was so thankful.

When graduation was over, everyone headed back home. Pot, Jenny and I were left to pack up and move on with our new lives. We all had done so well, and our future looked promising. Our college days, in Nashville, were over and we were far more grown up now, than we were when we first came. I had landed a job as an auditor for the City of Memphis and my training was to start in three weeks. Pot was now an official real estate agent, employed by one of the most prestigious real estate companies in the Mid-South. Her office was located in an exquisite office building in East Memphis overlooking the entire City of Memphis. Jenny was on her way to Connecticut to soon become Mrs. David Jerrod Jamieson. I knew Jenny didn't love David like that, but I believe she would have done anything to get away from Deacon Johns. She had also received a fantastic medical scholarship to one of the most prestigious Medical Centers on the East Coast. All her fees were paid; accompanied by a nice apartment and a monthly stipend, all provided by this Medical Center. Jenny will be a fantastic doctor.

God was with all three of us and it was up to us to believe in our selves, have faith, and go for the gusto. We were all in loving relationships with magnificent men and I could see all kinds of wonderful things happening for us.

****

A week passed, and Pot and I had to move out of the dorm. We still had a lot of stuff to pack. Pot was still away celebrating her graduation with her sweetheart and Jenny was already in Connecticut. I was so grateful for Matthew. He helped me pack all our things, put them in a small U-Haul truck, and volunteered to drive the U-Haul to Memphis. I couldn't let him do that though. I wasn't ready for him to go home with me, not just yet anyway. The truck wasn't very large, and I felt comfortable driving it myself. But he was afraid for me to get on the highway by myself, driving a U-Haul truck to Memphis.

"Ann," Matthew said. *"I can't let you drive this truck to Memphis by yourself."*

"I'll be okay," I told him as I got into the truck. *"Don't worry."* I said. *"I've driven to Memphis many times. I know that highway well, and I'm a very good driver."*

"I can't let you do it Ann; not alone anyway."

"I'll be okay, Matthew."

"No," Matthew said. *"I can't let you do it, okay! Just trail me home to my place, and tomorrow morning I'll trail you to Memphis. You can drive my car and I'll drive the U-Haul."* (Matthew raised his hands in the air as he made this promise.) *"You can sleep in my bedroom and I'll sleep on the sofa. I promise I will not touch you."*

"You promise?" I looked into his eyes as he gave his word.

"I promise." Matthew said.

Ann trailed Matthew to his place. He drove the U-Haul and she drove his car. When they got there, Matthew parked the truck and they drove to get something to eat. It had been a long day and Ann was very tired. She was also a little frustrated because Pot wasn't there to help her pack. But Matthew was a great help to her; he made her feel very special. They went to a quiet restaurant and had a nice dinner. The music was soft, the food was good, and the wine was excellent.

After dinner, they went back to Matthew's place. He was very kind. He showed Ann around and treated her like she was his best friend. Matthew showered in his guest bathroom while Ann locked the door to his bedroom and showered in his bathroom there.

"Everything smells so good." (Ann said to herself.) *"The towels and the bed sheets all smells like Matthew. Everything is so comfortable and clean. His bedroom is like heaven."*

Ann slept in Matthew's bed while he slept on the sofa in his great room. Ann was restless. She tossed and turned most of the night. During the middle of the night she got up, unlocked the bedroom door, and peered in at Matthew. He was all straddled out on the sofa, fast asleep. The blanket that covered him had partially fallen to the floor and he only wore the bottoms to his pajamas. Ann stood there looking at him. His arms and shoulders looked so strong. She went over and covered him with his blanket and softly snuggled in closely beside him on the sofa. Matthew was gently awaken and politely drew Ann closer to him.

"Hmmm, you okay?" Matthew asked very softly.

"Yes. I'm okay." I said. *"I just wanted to be near you."*

"Can I get you some warm tea or something?" He asked.

"No. I'm okay."

Ann moved her soft body closer to his and moved even more, trying to get closer to him. Matthew held Ann close and gently caressed her soft warm body. Ann's soft silk nightgown was the only thing between them. They began to kiss; over and over again. Their kisses were filled with passion and they both passionately desired each other. Matthew got up; politely picked Ann up and carried her into his bedroom; they were holding on to each other very tightly.

"Ann," he whispered softly. *"Is this okay?"*

"Yes." I said. *"It's okay."* And I held on tight.

Matthew skillfully took his time and gently entered Ann's warm body. He passionately entered her, giving her all of him, with as little pain as possible. Matthew was very easy with Ann and oh so gentle. As their bodies became one, Ann wanted those moments to last forever. She felt she didn't have a worry in the world. She was very comfortable having Matthew make love to her. After it was over, they held each other tightly all night long.

The next morning, they showered together, kissed passionately and made love all over again. Afterwards, Ann slept all morning like a newborn child. Matthew fixed a nice lunch, they ate, kissed passionately and made love again. Ann was physically drained. Although she loved every minute of their loving, she was exhausted. She also knew it was time for her to travel back to Memphis.

"Matthew, I've got to get out of here," I said softly, all wrapped up in Matthew's arms. *"I need to be on the road right now."*

"Yes, I know." He said. *"We better get a move on."*

Ann and Matthew showered together again; tidied up the place and got dressed. Suddenly there was a loud knock at the door. Matthew answered the door.

"Hey," Matthew said. (It was Pot.)

"Hey Matthew," Pot said. *"I apologize for disturbing you, but is Ann here?"*

Ann immediately rushed to the door.

"Where in the hell have you been?" I blurted out at Pot.

"And good afternoon to you too, Miss Ann." Pot said laughing. *"I went to the dorm. They said you had left. But I knew you weren't going to leave me. When I saw this U-Haul, I knew you were here."*

"I should have left your butt!" I said, fussing. *"You know you needed to help me pack! And you know we have to have this U-Haul back by eight o'clock tonight."*

"I know." Pot said, laughing. *"I'm here. So let's go.*

Matthew still wanted to drive the U-Haul to Memphis, but Ann wouldn't hear of it. She convinced him that Pot was there now and they would be fine driving to Memphis together.

Matthew and Ann said their goodbyes while Pot waited for Ann outside in the truck. Matthew and Ann promised to talk to each other every day until they were back in each other's arms again.

Pot and Ann had an enjoyable ride to Memphis. They talked about their sweethearts and how happy they were in their relationships. Ann told Pot it finally happened. Pot was happy for Ann and Pot thought Matthew was a swell guy. They talked about their new jobs and the area of the city they wanted to live in. Ann told Pot she had talked to Jenny and Jenny was all settled in. Life was good for the girls; just as good as Mama Sarah's sweet potato pie.

Chapter 10

Life, love, and the experiences of living

Finally, Ann and Pot were home from college. Their old friends filled them in on things that happened while they were away. But nothing had really changed. If anything, things had gotten worse. Many homes in parts of the neighborhood needed repairs, and many people were trying to move away, seeking nicer places to live. But besides all that, Mama Sarah and Kate were happy to have Ann and Pot home again.

Polly Mae was learning to cook and was ready to prepare many new dishes for the girls to try. Robert Lowell was very excited about Pot being home too. Telling everybody how proud he was of his little girl graduating from a college in Nashville, Tennessee. Nevertheless, one cannot truly say that Ann and Pot were totally happy to be home. They had outgrown that environment and it was really time for them to move on.

As the weeks passed, Ann and Pot were busy working and adjusting to their new jobs. Ann was so tired after work, that she came home, had dinner, did the dishes, read the newspaper, and went to bed.

Pot was living as a roommate with one of her new co-workers. A White girl, named Amy Andros, who lived in Germantown, Tennessee. Pot and Ann talked over the telephone everyday and saw each other one or two times a week. They kept in close touch with Jenny and Ann also talked often with Matthew. Matthew's Law Office was located in Nashville, but he was on an assignment in Washington D.C. and doing everything he could to work his way to Memphis.

The real estate market was booming and after three months, Pot had sold three houses. She loved her job and never dreamed she could make so much money. She was learning the business very well. Plus, she had the good looks, reliance, and a down to earth personality to become an exceptional real estate agent. Her sweetheart was very proud of her. He was happy to see her so happy.

Pot and Ann were moving on with their lives, just as Jenny was in Connecticut. Those four years away in college caused them to outgrow their surroundings and desire much more than just a modest lifestyle. Ann was getting bored with the old neighborhood and frequently grumbled to herself:

I have been home all these months and everyday everything is the same. Nothing has changed. Go to work, come home. Go to work, come home. I need something else to do. I need a few days off to take a short vacation. I'll ask Pot if we can slip away and go on a shopping spree in Atlanta. I'm so bored. I'm even tired of Mama Sarah. She's afraid for me to drive. She wants me in the house by midnight. She wants to know who I'm talking to on the telephone. My goodness! I need to get away. I need a break!

Ann arrived home from work that day, parked her car, and checked the mailbox. Among the mail was a wedding

**invitation from Jenny. Upon entering the house, Ann called
to Mama Sarah and Kate to share the invitation with them.**

"Mama; Aunt Kate" I called. They both came in where I was
at the same time.

"Hey Baby; what's the matter?" Mama Sarah asked.

"We have a wedding invitation;" I said. *"Jenny is getting
married."*

"What?" Mama Sarah and Aunt Kate said in unison.

*"Yep, she and David are getting married. The invitation says
they're getting married June 22, at four o'clock p.m., at Beth
Sinai Temple in Stamford, Connecticut."*

"Oh my Goodness;" Aunt Kate said, *"How nice!"*

"I guess she's really serious about this young man?" Mama
Sarah said. *"I wish them all the Blessings their minds can
conceive.*

"I have to call Pot right now." I said. *"This is so wonderful!*

**Ann telephoned Pot with the exciting news. Pot was very
surprised. They were both happy for Jenny. But Pot was a
little pissed; she wondered why she and Ann were not in the
wedding.**

"Why didn't she tell us Ann? Pot said. *I just talked to her a
couple of weeks ago and she never mentioned anything about
a wedding. We're supposed to be in her wedding! I'll be over*

as soon as I finish showing this property. We'll get her on the phone and find out what's going on. Ann, I don't know," Pot said. *"Are you sure Jenny is doing the right thing?"*

"Pot, let's not be negative. Jenny loves David. Let's give her our one hundred percent support."

"Okay," Pot said, *"If you say so. But if you ask me, I think she should think about this a little longer. But anyway, I'll be over as soon as I can."*

Ann and Pot talked to Jenny. The conversation was filled with moments of happiness and joy. The girls' laughter was even heard outside at Mama Sarah's house. Jenny explained the wedding ceremony to calm Pot down. Through the years, Jenny lost faith in her traditional Christian teachings and attached herself to a following with a more spiritual and truthful way of worshiping God. The wedding ceremony with this religious sect was a bit different, so Pot was okay with that. The girls had a happy evening chitchatting about Jenny's wedding. Ann and Pot were excited about a trip to the East Coast.

The news of Jenny's wedding spread fast and was talked about all over the neighborhood. Pot and Ann started shopping right away, looking for the perfect attire for this grand occasion.

Ann talked to Matthew and told him of her upcoming trip. He and Ann decided to spend a day together in New York City during Ann's visit.

Mama Sarah and Kate wouldn't be going. Neither of them had built up enough nerve to get on an airplane. Flying had become a part of Pot. She loved flying. She would fly with her

special guy anywhere he wanted to go and loved every minute of it.

Before Pot and I knew it, it was time for Aunt Kate and Big Daddy to take us to the airport. I was so excited. Mama Sarah had fixed a big lunch for us, but Aunt Kate wouldn't let us take it on the air plane. She explained to Mama Sarah that this was not a bus trip. Aunt Kate said they would serve food and drinks on the plane. I hope Mama Sarah was not offended.

The airport was big and crowded. I was nervous about my first time flying, but I had Pot to hold my hand. I knew everything would be all right with her by my side.

Flying felt good. It made me feel rich and important. Those few hours in the air elevated me to a higher level. I believe it even improved my vocabulary. By the time we landed, I believed I had started to talk "white." (Ann smiled to herself).

We were so happy to see Jenny. We acted a fool at the airport. We were hugging and jumping up and down like newly freed slaves. I wish we could always be together. We belonged together.

Pot and I were shocked at how Jenny and David lived. They were rich! The two of them were still in Med School and they drove Mercedes Benz automobiles. And the house they lived in was more elegant than the luxury hotel Pot and I had checked into.

Pot and I were happy for Jenny though. But with all this glamour and fine living, I could still feel something wasn't right. I could see in Pot's eyes that she felt the same way I did. But neither of us said anything. We couldn't question Jenny's livelihood, especially not on her wedding day.

The wedding was beautiful. It was a Jewish wedding and the wedding party included the groom's parents, the bride's parents and beautiful little flower girls. The venue was gorgeous. There was soothing classical music, huge beautiful live flower arrangements, and many important looking people.

Jenny's dress was stunning. All that white made the entire affair delightful and heavenly. David was escorted to the altar by his parents, and Jenny was escorted by Deacon Johns and Ms. Linda. Jenny marched around David and they both stated, *"I will, with the help of God."* It was so romantic.

David broke a water glass filled with water, then, poured wine into a new wine glass, and the two of them drank wine together from that same wine glass. I had never seen anything like that before. It was so beautiful. Their marriage contract was very unusual and they signed it right there during the wedding ceremony.

Photographs were taken by several photographers from all areas of the room. We danced and proposed toasts to Jenny and David's future. The food was delicious and the wedding cake was huge with several lifts between the tiers. Gifts were everywhere! The whole wedding ceremony was awesome, an event I will never forget. After the wedding, David had a limo drive me and Pot back to our hotel. We took food and wine to our hotel room and stayed up half the night talking about the great time we had.

The next morning, Jenny was to drive me and Pot to New York City. We planned to do a little shopping and sightseeing, and drive back to Stamford the next day. We hated to take her away from David so soon, but she didn't mind at all. She wanted to spend this time with me and Pot. We were there for only four days and we wanted to do so many things.

I really wanted to see Matthew. I hadn't seen him in over a year. I was so anxious to see him that my hands were ice cold. And many questions were going through my head. Does he still care for me? Will we make love? Has he outgrown this little country girl from the back woods of Tennessee?

Pot could see how uneasy I was. She told me not to be uptight at all. Pot said I was the best person in the whole world and that was a fact! She said I was better than one of Mama Sarah's butter milk biscuits, with her crazy self. She said my taste was better than Mr. Harthorn's mint tea. Pot said I was more beautiful than a rose in springtime. We laughed and talked until we fell asleep. I love Pot so much. She is such a good person. She means so much to me.

By the time we closed our eyes good, Jenny was knocking at the door. By noon, we were checking into our hotel in New York City.

New York City was beautiful. Everywhere I looked there was something wonderful to see. People were everywhere. There were tall buildings, vendors on street corners, restaurants, and shopping to no end. Everything was so fast and people were constantly moving, everywhere!

I talked with Matthew. He was driving from Washington D.C. to meet me at our Hotel. He was taking me to dinner. Pot had also talked to her sweetheart. She said he made it clear that he was missing her. Pot didn't seem to be bothered at all. She was happy just having fun with me and Jenny. I thought to myself, "Will Pot ever love anyone as much as she loved Willie Bill?"

We had a great time exploring New York. Jenny had us back at the Hotel at five o'clock so I could be ready to meet Matthew in the Hotel lobby at six. Jenny was a stickler for time, and so was Matthew. Neither of them were ever late.

I was rushing to be ready on time. I wanted to look my best to let Matthew know what he had been missing. I had lost a little weight, which made my twenty-five inch waistline look twenty-one inches. My dress fitted perfectly over my hips and my heels were six inches high. My hair was freshly bobbed and my cleavage was very enticing. I wanted Matthew to want me just as much as I wanted him.

At six o'clock, Matthew was downstairs. All three of us went down to meet him. Wow, was he looking good. He was made for a suit and tie. And as always, he publicly proclaimed tall, dark, and handsome; what a man!

He was happy to see all of us. We chatted for a moment, and the two of us were on our way. He flagged a taxi and in minutes we were at this cozy little spot in Harlem called Smoke. It was very romantic and the red lighting made everyone look sexy and appealing. The dinner and drinks were very good and the jazz band was awesome. We danced and Matthew held me close. I felt so good. I wanted him to lay me down right there and make love to me. I wanted him just that bad. I was truly in love with Matthew, but I would never let him know it. I would not make a fool of myself.

Matthew knew Ann seriously cared for him, but the timing just wasn't right. He cared for her too, but he had so much on his plate, he couldn't include a serious relationship at this time. The timing just wasn't right! He wanted the two of them to have a wonderful evening together and say goodbye until the next time. It was difficult for both of them.

"So, how's everything going in D.C., I asked him?"

After taking a sip from his drink, Matthew replied, *"Perfect, but busy. I have to burn the midnight oil three or four nights a week. Learning a lot though, but that's what it's going to take for me to be the best at what I do. D.C. is good, but I really prefer the quiet and peacefulness of the South."*

"Have you met any new friends; I asked?"

"Sure." He said. *"I'm meeting new people every day. That's my main purpose for being in D.C. Thurgood Marshall is the next person on my list. I want to get to know him personally. I want to know everything he knows about the law.*

Matthew, noticing a somber look on Ann's face, knew that enough had been said about him.

Okay," Matthew said. *"Enough said about me. What's been going on with you?"*

"Oh, not too much, just working every day and doing things with my family. Jenny's wedding was beautiful, and I'm really enjoying my time here. This part of the country is on the move and there's so much to see. I see now why everyone loves living here."

"Indeed." Matthew said, taking another sip from his drink. *New York, Philadelphia, D.C., this whole area is filled with history and education. All kinds of historical attractions, important landmarks, awesome museums, great people, great food, fantastic restaurants. The next time you're here I'm going to really show you around. Ann, they're playing our song. Shall we dance?"*

Ann looked at him with those big brown eyes, and said,

"Sure."

Their song was "Purple Rain Drops" by Stevie Wonder.

The evening went on and on, but, things didn't go as Ann hoped they would. She wanted Matthew to be totally elated to see her. She wanted him to take her in his arms, rush her away to a fancy Hotel, and make passionate love to her over and over again. But it didn't happen like that.

Matthew cherished Ann and didn't want to violate her in any way. He hadn't been faithful to her and he wanted her to know in her heart that he really cared about her and not just the treasure she carried between her legs. He wanted Ann to know that he wanted her in a true and honest way; when he could provide a good life for her; but now was not the right time.

They had a wonderful evening. Matthew took her back to the hotel; kissed her passionately and assured her that they would be together again very soon.

Ann watched Matthew until he was no longer in sight with tears in her sad eyes. She dried her eyes and went upstairs to Pot and Jenny. Pot and Jenny were in their pajamas, watching TV and eating popcorn. Ann came in and closed the door behind her.

"Ann, you're back; are you okay. Jenny asked? *Have you been crying?"*

Pot jumped up from the sofa and ran to comfort Ann. *"What did that Nigger do to you?"* Pot said. *"I'll put my foot in his ass, the son of a bitch!"*

"No." Ann said, speaking softly. *"It's not like that at all y'all. We had a wonderful time and it was hard for me to let him go.*

I believe Matthew loves me and I love him. I didn't want to let him go."

"Oh, Ann," Jenny said with passion in her voice.

The girls talked about Ann's evening and then went to sleep; ready to head back to Connecticut the next morning. Later that next day, Pot and Ann were on the air plane headed back to Memphis.

Kate and Big were to pick them up at the airport in Memphis, but when they arrived they were in for a big surprise. Polly Mae and Robert Lowell were there to pick them up and Robert was teaching Polly Mae how to drive.

"Mama," Pot asked her mother. *"Are you sure you know what you're doing?"*

"Yes girl." Polly Mae said. *"Robert has been teaching me to drive for a whole year now. As soon as I save enough money, I'm going to buy me a car."*

Pot and Ann were on pins all the way home. When they arrived at Mama Sarah's house, Polly Mae pulled up and parked like a top. Ann and Pot gave a sigh of relief. Several neighbors were sitting on the porch and standing in the yard, waiting for the girls to return. Everyone gave Polly Mae a loud hand clap for getting the girls home in one piece.

Everybody wanted to see the pictures of Jenny's wedding. After that, everybody went home and Ann turned in early to get some rest. She put on her pajamas, rolled her hair, turned the covers back, and got in bed.

"You've gone to bed already, baby?" Mama Sarah asked, standing at Ann's bedroom door.

"Yes ma'am." I said. *"I'm tired, and I have to work tomorrow."*

"Did you see your little boyfriend?" Mama Sarah asked.

"Yep"

"How did that go?" Mama Sarah asked as she came into Ann's bedroom and sat on Ann's bed.

"It went okay. I guess." I said. *"But I was hoping it would go better than it did. I didn't want to make a fool of myself. I didn't want to want him more than he wanted me. "Mama,"* I asked. *"How do you know how a man feels about you, and how do you know if he's the right one? I don't know what to think of my relationship with Matthew. I don't want to keep wasting my time."*

"Well baby, first of all," Mama Sarah said. *"Love is the greatest power in the universe. And when it's real, you'll know it. You'll see it in his eyes, "the eyes are the windows to your soul." And a man should tell a woman how he feels, but most of them don't know how to do that. It messes with their manhood. So, a woman has to mostly rely on her own inner spirit. Faith, love, and trust are spiritual gifts Ann. And our spirit protects us and reveals things to us. Your spirit will not fail you. Your spirit is the one true God, living within you. It will tell you if he is the one, and it will tell you if he isn't the one. But most of us don't listen. It's up to us to choose to obey or defy the signals our spirit sends. We must not drown those signals with fleshly desires to make the flesh feel good. We must be silent, we must listen, and we must obey. His eyes will always tell you if he's the one."*

160

Mama Sarah's words were comforting to Ann that night. As she continued to talk, Ann laid her head on Mama Sarah's shoulder and fell sound asleep. Mama Sarah laid Ann over on her pillow, covered her, and turned out Ann's light.

****

Before long, Ann was back to her same routine of going to work and coming home. Boredom was about to find its way back into her life again. She enjoyed her work and sometimes mingled with co-workers but that wasn't fulfilling. A couple of the guys at work were good for conversation, but no one struck her fancy like Matthew. She and Matthew wrote letters and talked over the telephone, but that was nothing like having him there.

Pot was busy with her real estate business, and her weekends were spent enjoying life with her sweetheart. Pot's busy schedule didn't leave much time for her to spend with Ann. Ann was happy for her though. Whatever this man was doing, it was making Pot happy; it was written all over her face. Sometimes she and Ann went for ice cream and had a good time laughing and talking about old times.

The holidays came and Mama Sarah had everyone over to decorate the Christmas tree as they drank hot chocolate spiked with homemade brandy. It was so much fun. Everyone saluted to the end of a great and wonderful year.

****

The morning of March 3, 1975 was a very cold morning. The wind was very high; it blew over everything that wasn't nailed down. Mama Sarah was up making coffee and getting some warm oatmeal for Ann's stomach before Ann took off for work. The telephone rang and it was Pot for Ann.

"Anna. Anna Two?" Mama Sarah called to Ann as Ann was hurriedly getting dressed for work.

"Ma'am," I answered, shouting so Mama Sarah could hear me over the music playing on WDIA radio.

"Pick up the phone." Mama Sarah said. *"It's Pot."*

"Yes ma'am." I picked up the phone. *"Hey girl, what's up?"* I said to Pot.

"Good morning, my number one best girlfriend." Pot said. *"I need you to do me a favor later today. And please say yes, I really need your help."*

"Sure," I said, *"If it doesn't snow. You know I hate driving in the snow."*

"Okay," Pot said. *"If it doesn't snow, I need you to help me show a house at five. Get here a little early and I'll show you everything you need to do."*

"Me? You sure you want me to do that? I don't know anything about showing a house Pot."

"It's easy Ann. You won't have a problem at all."

"Okay," I said. *"But I'm telling you now; I don't know anything about showing a house."*

"There's nothing to it." Pot said. *"I'm an expert in this field. See you at 4:30. Call me at 4 and I'll give you the address and tell you how to get there."*

All day long Ann wondered to herself, why Pot needed her to help her show a house. Ann was puzzled. She mumbled to herself throughout that whole day.

"Why in the world would Pot want me to help her show a house; I hope I'm dressed appropriately. I don't want to disappoint her."

All the anticipation caused Ann to have a lousy day. She made more mistakes at work that day than ever before. Four o'clock came and Pot told Ann to meet her at 4026 Shady Vista Road. She told Ann exactly how to get there. Ann drove and drove. Finally she made it. Pot was standing in the front yard waiting for her.

"What took you so long?" Pot said. *"I thought you were lost. I was worried sick."*

"I did get lost." I said, getting out of my car: *"You should have known that. You know I've never been out here before. I didn't know where in the hell I was."*

Pot laughed at Ann: *"You are so crazy, girl."* They then walked up the walkway to the front door.

"Wow," I said. *"What a beautiful home. Who's buying this home; White people or Black people? Can Black people live out here now?"*

"Girl, yes," Pot said, still laughing. *"Black people can buy anywhere they want to, if they have the money."*

"This home is beautiful Pot; absolutely beautiful!"

"Come on. Let me show you around." Pot took Ann on a tour of the house.

The four bedrooms, four and a half baths home was gorgeous. There were three bedrooms downstairs and one bedroom upstairs. There were huge master baths in all four bedrooms; walk-in closets, and vaulted ceilings. A large media room upstairs with a large balcony overlooking a beautiful backyard with a small tennis court and a paved walking track.

Downstairs was an open floor plan with large columns separating the great room and dining suite. There were huge windows, molding, trim, and chandeliers. There was carpet, and ceiling fans in all four bedrooms. A huge kitchen with a large bar and breakfast area; granite, and all new appliances. Plus, a large hearth room off the kitchen with a huge fireplace. There was a large patio, a two-car garage and much, much more. All located in an upscale, quiet neighborhood, next to a huge golf course. Ann was filled with awe throughout the whole tour.

"Pot, this is breathtaking. I've never seen a house like this before in Memphis!"

"Come on." Pot said, laughing. *"Let's go into the kitchen;"*

164

Pot went to the refrigerator, took out a bottle of wine and got two wine glasses from the cabinet. At that point, Ann didn't know what to think. She hoped Pot was not overstepping her authority by going in the refrigerator and helping herself to the home owner's wine. Pot opened the bottle, poured a glass for herself and one for Ann. Ann was surprised at the nerve of Pot.

Holding up her glass to toast with Ann, Pot said, *"It's ours Ann; yours and mine."*

"Ours;" I said. *"What do you mean it's ours?"*

"This is our house," Pot said. *"My sweetheart bought this house for me, and I had him to put your name on the deed right next to mine."*

"What! Are you serious? Pot, please, don't lie to me like that!

"He loves me Ann. He said if he can live in a big beautiful home, so can I. So he brought me out here, showed me this house, and told me it was mine. And you Ann, being the closest person in this world to me, I want you to live here too." Pot showed Ann the deed.

"Oh Pot; for real? I can't believe this. What are we going to do?"

Laughing, Pot said, *"We're going to live here."*

This was a great blessing for Pot and Ann. They hugged tightly and were as excited as two kids at Christmas. There was one drawback though. Pot made Ann promise not to tell anyone, not even Jenny. Pot said she wasn't ready to tell anybody about her sweetheart just yet. She said she would find a way to tell them later. They agreed to just say they were renting the house from one of Pot's clients.

Everything was going so well. Everybody loved the house. Mama Sarah, Kate, and Polly Mae were all trying to come up with enough money to buy Ann and Pot a nice bedroom suite. Mama Sarah went through all her new sheets, towels, and everything, packing boxes for Ann and Pot to take to the new house. Kate and Big paid for their telephones to be installed, and had a telephone installed in each bedroom. Pot's sweetheart gave her a credit card and told her to buy furniture for the whole house. For the next two weeks, Pot and Ann spent every evening, after work, shopping and buying for the new house. When they moved in, they were as happy as if they lived in paradise. Ann said a special prayer:

"I thank you God for all these good things happening for Pot and me. I am truly grateful for everything Pot's sweetheart has done for us. Bless him, my Wonderful Father; bless him with blessings beyond measure."

Pot and I checked out everything and found that everything was true. The house really was ours. Both our names were on the deed in the Shelby County Register's Office and the mortgage contract was stamped "Paid in full." We went to church the next Sunday to give special thanks to our Father God for such a wonderful blessing.

****

Living with Pot was easy. I just hated she was gone mostly every weekend. I was scared being in that big house by myself. I managed though. Between talking to Matthew, occasionally, and spending time with my co-workers, everything was cool. Plus, I always prayed for my royal prince to live in Memphis. I wasn't meeting anyone worth spending my time with, but I kept praying.

One evening after work, Pot brought her co-worker Amy Andros home with her. Pot was happy to show Amy around our beautiful home. I was a little jealous though. Pot was acting like Amy Andros was her best friend, and not me. I immediately snapped out of it, because Pot is a good person to everyone. She deserves every moment of her happiness.

The evening turned out good with lots of laughs. I made tacos; we kicked off our shoes, drank wine, ate tacos and listened to old school music. Pot and I taught Amy how to do the latest dances and boogie down. I was happy Pot had found another good friend; although I was still a little jealous.

After all that fun, Amy Andros never came over again. A few weeks later, Pot's supervisor called her in her office and told Pot they no longer needed her services and had to let her go. There was nothing Pot could do about it. I don't really know what happened, but I believe Amy Andros let hate, envy, and jealousy get the best of her. Pot was a good agent and I believe letting our hair down with Amy Andros didn't make a good impression. Mama Sarah always said, *"It's not good to let your left hand know what your right hand is doing."* Now I understand what she was trying to tell us.

Pot was very hurt. She cried so hard. I felt so bad for her. I assured her that I would pay every bill and keep food on the table until she was working again. But I believe Pot's main concern was she didn't want her sweetheart to think she was a failure. She didn't want to let him down.

Pot and I worked together diligently to find her another job. We even got Jenny involved. And as we should have known, Jenny made a few telephone calls, pulled a few strings, and within two weeks, Pot was hired by another agency. It was not an elaborate firm as before, but it was a very good company and Pot could work her way to the top. That damn Jenny is awesome!

In the meantime, just as things were settling down and getting back to normal, Jenny telephoned me and Pot to say she was pregnant. We were shocked! What in the world was Jenny going to do with a baby?

"Pregnant," Pot and I both said to Jenny at the same time.

"Jenny," I said, laughing. *"I knew you were going to lay your behind in that giant king sized bed and get a baby.*

Pot laughed too saying. *"If it's a girl, name her after me."*

Hell, naw," Jenny said, laughing. *"So she can come out twisting her little butt all over the place. Hell naw!"*

"Okay, okay," I said, *"let's name her Bell Bellevue so she can come out fighting;"* Then, we all had a good laugh.

Several weeks later, the ultrasound showed Jenny was having a girl. They were so excited. All Pot and Ann did was shop for the new baby girl. Jenny sent pictures every few weeks so Ann and Pot could see the baby grow. Mama Sarah knitted a blanket and Kate knitted a cap and bootees for the baby to wear home from the hospital. And early on Friday morning, November 18, 1975, at 3:20 a.m., Elizabeth Ann Potiece Jamieson was born, and they called her Lizzie. She was a beautiful child. Jenny and David were very lucky parents.

Mama Sarah said November 18 is a very good day. The same day Sojourner Truth was born. The birth dates of Charles Darwin, Walt Disney and Jackie Robinson. Mama Sarah said this meant that Jenny's baby girl was going to be strong, determined, and very ambitious.

Mama Sarah sent the baby a Christmas box and made everybody send the baby a present. The box was so big, it took all of us to wrap it and get it to the post office in time for Christmas. Mama Sarah said she couldn't wait for me and Pot to get married and have babies. She said she was going to spoil them rotten. Pot looked at me with sad eyes. I gave her two thumbs up and a big smile to let her know she was a strong, magnificent woman with an outstanding future.

Pot and I wanted to visit Jenny and the baby right away, but the new realty company Pot worked for had her swamped. She worked six and sometimes seven days a week. The little time she did have off was spent with her darling sweetheart.

Finally, in the following month of March, Pot scheduled a long weekend off and we flew out to see Jenny. I didn't tell Mathew I was coming. If he was serious about seeing me, he would take time from his busy schedule and come to Memphis to me. This trip was for Jenny. Pot and I both could hear in her voice that she needed us.

Little Lizzie was almost four months old when Pot and I first saw her. She was so cute and fat. I could have played with her all day long. I wish I could have said the same about her mother. I was worried about her. She didn't look good at all. She was pale and skinny, and her hair was breaking off. And Lizzie was only three months old and Jenny was pregnant again. That damn David; he didn't even give her stitches time to heal. I guess he has succeeded at not letting her have her own career. He knew Jenny would be a much better physician than he is; he doesn't want to compete with her. So he's keeping her pregnant and tied down with children.

Pot and I were shocked when Jenny told us she was pregnant again. She can barely handle one baby, and now she going to have two. I know David is her husband, and I don't want to talk against him, but he's not good for her. She needs to get the hell away from him now!

Ann and Pot stayed with Jenny five days and during that time David was never home. The nanny kept little Lizzie while Jenny drove Pot and Ann to the airport. Jenny hated to see them leave. There was nothing Ann and Pot could say to make their departure easy. They both promised Jenny they would return to be with her for the birth of the new baby. Jenny cried when Pot and Ann got on the airplane.

Pot and I took a taxi home from the airport. Neither of us talked much. We sat silently, looking out the window, thinking of what we could do to make life better for Jenny. Jenny appeared to be very unhappy and that made me and Pot sad. I prayed that Jenny would have changes in her life very soon.

Pot's sweetheart sent a car for her as soon as we got home. I guess his hormones were getting the best of him. He kept Pot with him mostly every night. Some nights she didn't come home at all. She went to work from his place. Pot said he had a Penthouse Apartment in Downtown Memphis and that's where she would be. She gave me the telephone number there, but I wouldn't dare call. I wouldn't want them to panic due to the telephone ringing, thinking it may be his wife calling. Yes, I believe he's married. Pot just hasn't told me yet. There are red flags everywhere alluding to his being a married man. I know Pot see them as plain as I do, but what the hell, I guess every Jack Kennedy desires a Marilyn Monroe.

I was lonesome at home by myself, but I didn't bitch about it. I just needed to make some new friends. Some nights, on weekends, I stayed at Mama Sarah's, especially when she cooked greens. She always enjoyed having me. We would talk about everything: men, politics, the Bible. Sometimes she would read the Bible out loud to me. At times, I would wake up in the middle of the night and she would be sitting up in her bed, reading. Mama Sarah had all kinds of books. Medical books, books on herbs, science books, books on astrology, and books on stuff I had never heard of before. She loved Black history. She believed the Black race was the superior race, but our supernatural perception and courageous spirit had been watered down by mixing with other races. At times, some of that stuff Mama Sarah talked about sounded so ridiculous, I just stayed at home. At home, I could listen to good music and reminisce about my good times with Matthew. I wanted him so bad, but it was evident that he didn't want me, so I had to live with that. We would write letters and talk over the telephone on special occasions, but I wouldn't dare let him know I was lonely for him.

I always talked over the telephone with Jenny too. I did everything I could to keep her spirits up. I often wondered what happened to us. It seemed that neither of us was truly happy. All those good things we had going for us; yet, we were still longing for that unspeakable joy to make our lives complete.

Chapter 11

Why look back; you can only go forward

Months passed and the new baby came. Jenny was scheduled to have the baby November 21, 1976, and thank God I was there, the baby came right on time. Pot couldn't be there. Her sweetheart had taken her to Sweden to celebrate her birthday. The baby was a beautiful baby boy. I hoped Jenny wouldn't name him after David, but she did.

Pot talked to us several times over the telephone. She was delighted about the baby's birth and promised to bring all of us a nice souvenir upon her return. She sounded good and said she was having a great time. She said Stockholm was one of the most colorful cities she had ever seen. She said the beautiful harbors and exotic museums made it the perfect place for lovers.

I passed on contacting Matthew again. I forced myself not to think about him and enjoyed my time with Jenny and the children. David and his parents were happy about a boy child. They gave Jenny their 100% support, but I could still see in Jenny's eyes that she wanted to go home to Memphis. Regardless of how ruthless and cruel Deacon Johns had been, I felt in my heart she still wanted to go home.

I stayed with Jenny three days. I then flew to Detroit to spend Thanksgiving with my parents. They were so happy to see me especially my father. I believe he has always felt that I don't truly love him, but that's not true at all. I have really grown and I have a great deal of love and respect for my father. He's a great man, and has provided a good life for my mother and my brothers. Amy Mae and those boys are his life, and I respect that.

Thanksgiving dinner was very good. I was surprised to know my mother was a great cook. My brothers have beautiful girlfriends. Mark's girlfriend is White, and as for Mama Sarah, that's going to take a little getting used to.

I stayed in Detroit four days and everyday Mama Sarah telephoned asking me when I was coming home. She said she didn't want me to get caught in Detroit in bad weather; but, I think she was missing me more than anything else.

I enjoyed my time with Amy Mae. She took me everywhere. I got Motown T-shirts for everybody back home. I told her I was planning a Thanksgiving Dinner in Memphis next year, so everybody could come. She was elated to hear that.

Everybody went to the airport with me. Amy Mae asked if I could return for New Year's Eve or the fourth of July. I promised her I would think about it. My dad hugged me real tight and kissed me on my forehead. I could see my parents really loved me, more than I ever dreamed they did.

When my plane landed in Memphis, Mama Sarah was right there at the airport with Aunt Kate and Big Daddy, fussing at me for not having a headscarf on my head. She wanted me to spend the night at her house, but I told her I needed to get home and check on the house.

They took me home and we all went inside to make sure everything was okay. I walked them to the car and said goodnight. Before I could hardly lock the door hind me, the telephone rang.

"Hello." I said. It was Matthew.

"Ann!" He said. *"I've been trying to reach you for days. Is everything okay?"*

"Sure. How are you?" I asked him.

"I'm good; just missing you. I called to wish you and your family a happy Thanksgiving, but I didn't get anybody."

"Oh, I apologize for that Matthew. I went to Detroit to spend Thanksgiving with my parents."

"And your Grandma let you do that?" Matthew said laughing.

"You are so awful." I said. *"She telephoned everyday asking when was I coming home."*

"Well, I know she wants you home for Christmas, so can you come to D.C. and spend your birthday with me? I'll send for you."

"Oh Matthew, that's so sweet. But I don't know. I just got back and I'll have to see how things are at work. I would love to come, but I'll have to let you know."

"Good." Matthew said. *"I'll make plans so we can have a great time."*

Ann didn't know what to do. She really wanted to see Matthew. But she didn't want to seem gullible and available anytime he wanted her. She didn't necessarily want to play hard to get, but she did have morals and her character to think about. Ann knew if she went to D.C., sex would be involved. And she had decided she wouldn't make love with Matthew

ever again if they were not planning to be married. That one thing alone gave Ann the courage to tell him *"No."*

Although Ann didn't spend her birthday with Matthew, she had a fantastic day after all. Mama Sarah cooked her a wonderful birthday dinner and she and Pot hung out at the old neighborhood corner bar. They saw many of their old throwback friends from the old neighborhood. They drank daiquiris, and laughed all evening long. They had a wonderful time. Matthew was a bit disappointed, but he got over it. He sent Ann flowers and a wonderful gift for her birthday. They also exchanged gifts through the mail for Christmas.

****

The New Year brought Jimmy Carter as the new president and hope for a new beginning. Ann brought the New Year in on her knees, praying with Mama Sarah, while Pot counted down the New Year in Times Square with her sweetheart. Jenny was home with the kids and David was away on a business trip. It was so cold outside in Memphis, until mostly everybody stayed home, warming themselves around a nice warm fire.

Nineteen seventy six was a good year, everybody's alive, healthy, and happy. Jenny's new baby is here and I'm looking forward to spending more time in 1977, getting to know him and Lizzie too.

I have so much to do during this year, with the Thanksgiving Dinner and all. I can hardly wait for Mama Sarah to see all her children. She hasn't seen many of them for a very long time. Aunt Louise, Aunt Bell, and Uncle Robert will be happy to be home again. I can't wait to see the joy in Mama Sarah's eyes. But right now, I'm going to pop some popcorn and watch the first episode of Roots. I hope Pot comes home so we can watch it together.

****

The months in 1977 went by so fast. Before the girls knew it, it was August. Elvis' death on August 16 brought a great sadness over the entire City of Memphis and around the world. Black people, White people, the young, and the old, were sad over Elvis' passing. His death even brought tears to Mama Sarah's eyes. Ann, Mama Sarah, Kate, and Big all went to Graceland to join other Elvis fans morn Elvis's passing.

Mama Sarah said Elvis was a good man. She loved all of his music. She hated to see him leave Lisa Marie and Priscilla alone. Mama Sarah experienced that same situation once upon a time in her own life and she didn't want to see it happen to anyone else. Mama Sarah believed all children needed their father in their lives forever. She said Memphis would always remember Elvis because Elvis always remembered Memphis.

****

During the next few weeks, Ann was diligently at work getting everything arranged for her upcoming Thanksgiving Dinner. She contacted caterers, a bartender, and decorators. Plus, she was very busy getting the guest list together. She really needed Pot's help very bad.

The weeks came and went and before Ann knew it, time had gotten away from her. The more she planned, the more she thought of things she needed to do. Ann needed input from someone else and hoped that person would be Pot. But Pot,

like always, had plans of her own. She refused to waste her time planning a dinner for people she thought wouldn't appreciate it anyway. She loved traveling with her sweetheart and every time his plane took off, she was trying to be on it.

One evening, after work, Ann drove up at home and Pot's car was parked in the garage. Ann hurried inside, calling Pot's name as she entered the door from the garage.

"Pot, Pot." I called, while putting down the things I brought in from my car.

"Yeah," Pot said. *"I'm in here, trying to find my orange scarf."*

"Hey:" I said, as I joined Pot in her bedroom, *"you going out?"*

"Uh-huh, my honey is sending a car for me."

"Sending a car for you? How long are you going to be gone?"

"Not long; just a couple of days."

"Dang Pot, a couple of days: Sometimes a couple of days for you can turn into two or three weeks! And I was hoping you would help me with the final plans for our Thanksgiving dinner."

"Our Thanksgiving dinner;" Pot shouted. *"I didn't tell you I was going to help you with that!"*

"You know I need someone to help me." I followed Pot as she walked through the house preparing to leave. *"Since it's here, at our house, I thought you would take a little time to help."*

"Well you thought wrong!" Pot shouted. *"I have my own stuff to do. Hire somebody to help you! Get Aunt Kate. I'll help you pay her. But don't include me in getting nothing together. This is your party, not mine!"*

Ann and Pot's little disagreement turned into a brief shouting match and before they knew it, their conversation almost got out of hand.

"Sometimes I don't know what's wrong with you Pot. This man has taken you over. You put your family, your job, and everything on the back burner for him. Sometimes you act like your family doesn't exist. Is this love Pot, or is he just using you for his bed wench!"

Ann was shocked herself to hear those words come out of her mouth. Pot stood and looked at Ann with hurt in her eyes. Ann just stood there staring at Pot as if she was mad as hell.

"Do you think our beautiful home, this luxury furniture, our cars, and even that damn job you have came from a fuck in the night? Is that what you think Ann? Is that what you think! If that's all it took, I could have had all this shit and more a long time ago. And, what about that two bit shyster lawyer you sit around looking like a fool and moping over! While he struts up and down the East Coast in his five hundred dollar Brooks Brothers' Suits, laying every whore he can persuade out of her panties! What do you call that Ann? Is that love, or does he just love a whole lot of bed wenches?"

Ann screamed out crying and ran to her bedroom. Pot didn't mean those words and neither did Ann. They both let this shouting match go a little too far. Pot went to Ann's room to

apologize. Pot knocked on Ann's door and entered Ann's bedroom.

"Ann, I'm sorry." Pot said. *"I didn't mean those words. I was just being mean. What you said hurt me and I was just firing back. I didn't mean to hurt you."*

I dried my eyes as I said, *"I'm sorry too Pot; Please forgive me. Maybe these men are a bit much for us. We need to talk to Mama Sarah. She can help us work these things out."*

"No!" Pot shouted, *"We can't talk to Mama Sarah about our men. Do you think I want her to know I'm seeing Atticus Sharp? No, I do not! And if you tell her, I promise you Ann, I'll kill myself!"*

Suddenly the telephone rang. Pot walked over and answered it. It was Pot's sweetheart's driver. A car was waiting for Pot.

"Yes. I'll be right down," Pot said. *"A car is here for me."* Pot told Ann. *"I've got to go. If you need me, you know how to reach me."*

Pot got her overnighter and purse and hurried to the waiting car. As Pot got into the car, Ann stared at her from a window. You could see in both their eyes that they were sorry. The car drove off and Ann stood there looking up at the stars from the window, thinking to herself:

I know this man loves Pot. I know he does. I don't know why I said what I said. He gives Pot everything and takes her to so many wonderful places. He has to be a good man. Pot is so blessed. I guess I'll go to bed and get some sleep. I'll work on the Thanksgiving celebration tomorrow.

Things around 4026 Shady Vista Road was reserved and quiet for the next few weeks. Although Pot and Ann were sorry for the things they said, they still only talked to each other when they just had to. They both tried to avoid each other as much as possible.

Ann managed to get everything done, and things were looking pretty good for Thanksgiving. Mama Sarah was baking a leg of lamb, Kate was preparing ham, turkey and dressing, and the caterers were handling all the rest, even the homemade rolls. The decorators had done a fabulous job on the house, inside and out. Everybody invited had decided to come, even Jenny and the kids. David was going to be away on a business trip.

****

Before long, November 24, 1977, had finally come. It was a wonderful day, cool and crisp, and at seven o'clock a.m., Pot and Ann were on their way to the airport to pick up Jenny and the kids. Neither of them said very much to each other, but they both were excited about Jenny coming home.

The airplane arrived on time, and Ann and Pot were right there waiting as Jenny and the children entered the airport from the plane. When Jenny and the children appeared, hugs and kisses went on and on. Ann and Pot were so happy to see them. The children had really grown. Lizzie was the perfect little lady and DJ had just started to walk.

181

"Oh Jenny," I told her. *"The children are so pretty. I'm so happy to see y'all. I love y'all so much."*

"Me too," Pot said. *"I'm so happy y'all are here."*

"I've missed y'all too," Jenny said, hugging Ann and Pot both at the same time while Ann held DJ. *"What's wrong?"* Jenny asked out of nowhere. Looking at them, Jenny could feel something was wrong. *"What's the matter with y'all?"*

"Nothing," Pot answered.

"Well," I said. *"We've been fussing about a few things, but we'll get over it."*

"Sure you will!" Jenny insisted. *"It's Thanksgiving, and I'm home! I don't know what the problem was, but it's gone now. So hug and make up right now. Hug and make up,"* Jenny put Pot and Ann's arms around each other and they hugged.

Pot and Ann hugged each other and felt one hundred percent better.

"Good," Jenny told them. *"Now I'm ready for the Feast, the Booze, the Music, and a Happy Thanksgiving! I'm home! And I know now, this is where I want to be."*

They got the luggage and happily started the drive home.

"I'm so happy to be home," Jenny said again. *"I thought I would never get here. And guess what you guys?"*

Pot and Ann had a surprised look on their face wondering what Jenny was about to say.

"David is working on opening an office here, in Memphis. Hopefully, in the next year or so, we'll be home for good."

"Whew." I said. *"For a minute there I thought you were about to say you were pregnant again!"* We all laughed.

The girls were so happy together. They were a family again, if only for a short while. Jenny loved the house. She and the children felt right at home.

The Thanksgiving Dinner was great. Everybody came and it was a very good day. They talked about old times; played cards, danced, took pictures and had a wonderful time. Ann stood around in awe, so grateful to have everyone there. She prayed a silent prayer as she watched everyone enjoy themselves:

Thank you so much My Wonderful Father God for this wonderful day. Everybody is here. I'm so thankful for that. Amy Mae and Charlie Murphy, Mark and Ben with their girlfriends, Mama Sarah, Aunt Kate and Big Daddy, Uncle Robert and his Japanese wife with their son. He's so cute. He looks more Black than Japanese though. Aunt Bell looking good with Mr. Bridgeforth and he look good too. I guess being with Aunt Bell helped him. He looks so happy. I hate Ms. Pig died, but all their children turned out good. They all migrated to California and are living good lives. I guess Mama Sarah was so glad to see Aunt Bell, she forgot all about choking Aunt Bell's tongue out of her mouth. Aunt Louise's sporting a four thousand dollar Mink Coat, and her boyfriend, wow, he's so handsome. Ms. Polly Mae and Mr. Lowell look so happy together. Ms. Addie Mae, Mr. Walter, and everyone else look happy too. Most of all, thank you Father for Jenny and the children.

Everybody loved our home. They whispered one to another, wondering how two young girls could afford such an expensive place to live. I was glad Jenny was there with the babies. The babies held everyone's attention and kept their minds from wondering how Pot and I could afford to live in our beautiful home.

The help did a fantastic job on everything. We had wine, champagne, and we danced the night away. I wish Matthew could have been here. Everybody asked about him. I lied about his whereabouts. I was too ashamed to tell them he couldn't fit this delightful engagement into his busy schedule.

After Thanksgiving we had enough love among us to last forever. I was happy to see Mama Sarah with all her children. It made her so happy. Everyone returned to their homes safely and looked forward to our next family gathering.

****

Now that everything was over, Pot and I were back to our usual routine. We were closer now than ever. She was home more often and we hit the gym two or three times a week trying to rid ourselves of the pounds we put on during the Holidays. That's where I met Allen Fulton, a very nice guy. He was very good-looking too. He had a nice position at Harvester, a nice car, and was buying his own home. I was very impressed, but I still wanted Matthew. Matthew and I still talked over the telephone; he still sent flowers and money for me to go shopping, but I promised myself I wouldn't sleep with him again until we were planning to be married. That's why I wouldn't go to him in D. C. Pot said her sweetheart would fly me there anytime, for free, but I wouldn't accept his offer. I held true to my commitment to myself. As for our relationship, it was all, or nothing.

Ann loved Matthew, but she was determined to stand as a strong woman. She couldn't see herself crawling to him, on his terms, begging for his love and affection. Ann went on with her life and believed that someday she would be in a loving relationship and truly happy.

Ann and Pot were grateful for their blessed lives. The Thanksgiving gathering brought them closer together and gave them a better understanding of how love and respect is needed in a family. They traveled more together and went back to Connecticut a couple of times to visit Jenny.

Pot loved traveling and was away many weekends with her sweetheart, leaving Ann more time to spend with Allen Fulton. Ann struggled to keep Allen at arm's length because she still loved Matthew. She didn't want to lead Allen on. She wanted to be truthful and real. She felt Allen deserved that because he really was a swell guy. Ann tried hard to fall in love with Allen, but it just wouldn't happen.

****

Spring came, then winter, then fall, then Spring again, and before long, two years had passed. Early one Saturday morning while Ann was busy washing and folding towels, the telephone rang. (Ring, ring, ring...) It was Jenny.

"Hello." I said, answering the telephone.

"Ann." Jenny said.

"Hey Jenny, What up? What're you doing up so early?"

"I couldn't sleep." Jenny said. *"I'm so happy. I couldn't wait to call you."*

"What!" I ask. *"What is it?"*

"Ann, we're moving back to Memphis!"

"For real; oh Jenny when?"

"Real soon, like in a few weeks. David has a contract to start a new Pharmaceutical Research Center there."

"Oh Jenny I'm so happy." I said. *"I can't wait to tell Pot. Oh Jenny, that's great news."*

"I'm happy too;" Jenny said. *"I can't wait; I'm already packing my bags. We'll be there in two weeks to look at a house. I'm so happy Ann!"*

Ann, Pot and Jenny were all excited. They talked over the telephone almost everyday laughing and giggling, planning things to do when Jenny move home. Everyone was happy about Jenny and her family moving back to Memphis. Deacon Johns looked happy too.

****

Everything lined up perfectly. David's research center opened, and two weeks after that, Jenny, the kids, the nanny,

and the dog, all joined David at their new home in Collierville, Tennessee. Pot was away with her sweetheart, but Ann was driving to Collierville to see them, jubilant about Jenny being home again.

"Pot is going to love this area of Shelby County; it's nice out here in Collierville. (Ann arrived at Jenny and David's home.) Wow! Pot's going to freak out over this house they've bought. There's one thing about David, he's always going to go first class. The top of the line; that's the kind of guy he is. Smart, classy, extravagant, and all the other words you can think of to define rich. And they are my friends! My friends! Now that Jenny's home, maybe I'll meet one of David's rich friends, fall in love, and get married. This could be a new beginning for me too."

Ann arrived at Jenny's new home and spent the whole day with them. The house was most lovely: flower gardens in the back yard, a beautiful pool, a play area for the kids, and servants. Things most Black people dream about. And even with this dream life, Jenny still appeared to be unhappy. Ann didn't know what to think. She was hoping Jenny wasn't pregnant again. Then again, Ann thought, so what if she is. They have plenty of money and their children are the best children in the world. Ann couldn't understand it. She wondered how someone with so much could be so unhappy! What could be wrong?

After a few weeks, things did get better. Ann, Jenny and Pot were glued together. Shopping, eating out at nice restaurants, and when David was out of town, Jenny and the children spent nights at Pot and Ann's home. All three of them were perfect little mothers to the children and loved every minute of it.

****

A year passed and Halloween came. Children were everywhere, going door to door for Halloween treats. Pot and I rushed home after work to be ready for the little Ghost and Goblins. We dressed in our Halloween costumes and passed out candy, waiting for Jenny and the kids to come.

"Pot, here they come," I called to Pot, when I saw Jenny drive up.

I hurriedly closed the door so Lizzie and DJ could ring the doorbell. *Ring. Ring.* They rang the door bell and I opened the door.

"Trick or treat?" Lizzie and DJ said.

Pot and I pretended to be afraid of the ghost and witch at our door. Pot and I screamed and trembled with fear as we gazed upon the ghost and witch standing there. Lizzie and DJ took off their mask and laughed to let us know it was really them. It was so much fun.

****

November 12th came and Pot was off again with her sweetheart to celebrate her birthday. David was also out of town, so Jenny and I decided to do a little Christmas shopping. I felt this would give Jenny a little time away from the children to enjoy herself. She was with them constantly, and they had a nanny. I'm not a parent, but I believe being away from your children a few hours a day is healthy for you. Jenny looked stressed most of the time; but she always said she was okay. But I knew she was lying. Something was troubling her and this would give me a chance to drag it out of her. Plus, we could do some shopping for our own birthday, and we did. We shopped all afternoon, then, stopped for a bite to eat. We stopped at this nice little restaurant in the mall. I had a hoagie, fries and a shake. Jenny had coffee.

"I'm ready for this." I said. *"I didn't eat any breakfast this morning. Did you?"* I asked Jenny.

"Now you know I don't eat breakfast." Jenny responded.

"You should." I told her. *"You're a doctor. You know breakfast is the most important meal of the day. And you need to eat because your behind is really skinny."*

"Can we talk about something else?" Jenny said. *"I don't want to talk about my behind. Please, let's change the subject."*

"Okay. Let's talk about why you seem to be so worried and depressed all the time. You're rich, married to a wonderful guy, and have two perfect children. And you walk around acting like it's the end of the damn world! "What's the hell wrong with you?"

"Stop overreacting Ann! Nothing is wrong with me."

"Look heifer, look at me; don't give me that shit. You know I know your ass. Now tell me what's the hell going on with you and don't tell me it's nothing." I starred directly into Jenny's face, waiting for the truth. Teary eyed, she finally broke down and talked to me.

"Oh Ann," Jenny whispered. *"I want to leave David."*

"You want to leave David? What's wrong?"

"I don't know." Jenny said, with tears in her eyes. *"So much has happened and things are still happening. I can't take it anymore. I'm afraid for me and I'm afraid for my children too."*

"Things like what?" I asked. *"What's the hell going on, Jenny. Tell me!"*

"I can't Ann. It's so much. I don't even know where to begin."

"Jenny, you know you can talk to me and Pot too. We want to help you."

"No." Jenny said. *"Let's not involve Pot. I should have never said anything! I guess I just want my own practice. I don't know how to go about it and David feels there's no need for me to work, but I want to work. I want my own practice."*

"Well, do it Jenny! You know you can do anything, if you put your mind to it. Tell David to go to hell! I know he's your husband, but God gave you this life; do some of the things you want to do. I say, go for it. I'll be right here by your side, supporting you one hundred percent."

"I know you will Ann. And I'm going to do it! Damn David's ass. By God, I'm going to do it. I needed this encouragement. I'm smart and I'm strong; I know I can do it. Thanks Ann. I really need your support. Thank you for helping me to realize that I can do this." Jenny placed her hand over Ann's hand as a gesture to say thank you.

All kinds of evil things were going on in Jenny and David's marriage. She had supported her husband in all his evil doings, and now she wanted out. But for David, this was only the beginning. His criminal behavior of blackmail and falsifying medical records was nothing compared to what he had in mind this time. His dream was to have every person in this country on prescription drugs; the young, the old, Black, White, rich, and poor. The more medical prescriptions purchased each day, the more capital for David's skyrocketing bankroll. And to David, wealth meant power, and he would do anything to have it, even commit murder.

****

Weeks passed and Jenny promised herself, after the first of the year, she was leaving David and starting out on her own. David, being the manipulating lowlife that he was, could sense something wasn't right. He could feel Jenny was unhappy and wanted to leave him. So he played the game of cunning and swindling her to stay by his side. Even though he didn't truly love Jenny, she was a good mother to his children; and, an important player on his team. Jenny would do anything David asked. He believed she was faithful to him. He trusted her and he depended upon her to help get the hard jobs done. He couldn't let her go.

On the weekend of January 24, 1981, David had their nanny fly the children to Hartford to spend the weekend with his parents. He and Jenny would be home alone and he was determined to play the roll of a loving husband to keep Jenny by his side. It was late, snowing outside, and they were both in the family room watching TV.

"Jenny," David said. *"Come over here on the sofa with me."*

"For what," Jenny replied. *"I'm comfortable over here where I am."*

David stood up, walked over to Jenny, and sat down next to her. He started to stroke her hair affectionately as he kissed her softly on her face and neck.

"Stop, David!" Jenny said. *"I don't feel like that right now."*

"I need you, baby." David whispered in a low soft breathy voice. *"That's why I sent the kids away. I need you so much."*

Before Jenny could say "stop" again, David had put his mouth over Jenny's mouth and started to kiss her passionately.

"I've been missing you so much." He whispered softly. *"Please Baby, don't say no. I love you Jenny. I want you so much. I want us to have another baby right now Jenny, right now."*

Before Jenny could force him off of her, he started kissing her deeply with passion, and in minutes he had opened her legs and entered her right there on the sofa. Jenny just gave in and responded.

They stayed snowed in the whole weekend and made love several times. But as far as having another baby, Jenny had taken care of that a long time ago.

Monday couldn't come fast enough for Jenny. She was happy to pick up the nanny and the children from the airport. After spending the weekend with David, she was confused. She didn't know if she should leave him or if she should stay. She loved David and wanted the children to have both parents in the home, but in reality, she was miserable under the same roof with him.

When Jenny and the children arrived home from the airport, David was in their bedroom packing a suitcase. Lizzie and DJ ran into the house, rushing to their daddy.

"Daddy, Daddy!" Lizzie and DJ called to their daddy.

"Hey, Buckaroos," David said, picking them up at the same time; kissing them on the forehead.

"Daddy missed you," he told them as he let them down.

"Where're you going Daddy?" Lizzie asked.

"Daddy's going on a short business trip. But I'll be back in a couple of days, and we'll have lots of fun, okay?" He said as he tickling them.

"Okay." Lizzie said. DJ nodded his head, okay, too. *"DJ, let's get Skip."* Lizzie said. They both ran outside to the back yard looking for Skip, their dog.

"Where're you going?" Jenny asked David.

"I've got to make a quick run to Nashville." David said. *"Harrison called. Our accounts have been frozen for some crazy reason. We can't make payments for supplies. I'm driving up to see what the hell's going on."*

193

"You need me to come with you?" Jenny asked.

"Naw, I think it's something minor. I'll be back in a day or two." David kissed Jenny on the lips, carried his luggage to the car, and drove off.

****

David arrived in Nashville in less than three hours. He went straight to his Accountant's office and contacted his bank. His Bank informed him that his accounts had been frozen by Matthew Middleton of Myles, Middleton and Carr Law Firm, in Washington, D.C. The Bank official explained that the accounts were frozen due to a failure to fulfill an indebted obligation for medical supplies provided by Meds, Inc. David was furious, outraged and extremely angry. He immediately telephoned Matthew's Law Firm. The receptionist answered and transferred him to Matthew.

"Myles, Middleton and Carr, may I help you?" The receptionist answered.

"Yes, Matthew Middleton, please." David replied.

"One moment please." The call was forwarded to Matthew.

"Attorney Middleton," Matthew answered.

"Matt," David said. *"This is Jamieson man. What's the meaning of this shit, man?"*

"Mr. Jamieson, good afternoon Sir;" Matthew replied. *"I should be asking you that question."*

194

"Don't play games with me Nigger!" David said. *"You know what the fuck I'm talking about!"*

Matthew kept his cool. *"I apologize if I have offended you Sir, but I'm representing Johnson White of Meds, Inc. And Mr. Jamieson, Meds, Inc. has ended all business with you as of yesterday! You have thirty days to pay Meds Inc. two million dollars, or we will move forward to bring charges against you and your Corporation!*

"Charges against me," David shouted. *"Are you crazy nigger? What in the hell are you talking about?"*

"Mr. Jamieson, I'm talking about blackmail, extortion, bribery, misuse of authority as a medical doctor, tampering with medical evidence, corruption. Do you want to hear more?"

"Man you're crazy!" David shouted. *"Whatever Johnson has told you, he's lying. You don't have a got-damn thing on me. I demand that you release my assets immediately or you will hear from my attorney. You understand that; you worthless backstabbing son of a bitch! Release my fucking assets right now!"*

David slammed the telephone down and immediately telephoned William Russell Knight, his attorney. David was in an uproar as he informed Attorney Knight of his situation. Attorney Knight was very calm and managed to relieve David of his fears.

"David, calm down," Attorney Knight told him. *"This guy's bluffing. He's trying to frighten you. Don't worry. You have an essential medical establishment, necessary for the health*

and well-being of human life. He can't shut you down that easy. I'll file a preliminary injunction and release this freeze within hours. We will then request a Court Hearing and require Meds, Inc. to prove they have a legal right to freeze your assets and put an end to this nonsense. Who is this shyster anyway?"

"Good," David said, as he breathed a sigh of relief. *"Go ahead Russell and do that. I'll let my office know we'll be back in business in a couple of days. The attorney is Matt Middleton of Myles, Middleton, and Carr in D.C. They also have an office here in Nashville."*

"Very good," Attorney Knight said. *"I'll get on it right away. And David, I'm your attorney, let me handle the legal matters, okay?"*

"Sure." David said. *"Thanks man."*

David didn't tell Attorney Knight everything. He told him the money was a loan and Johnson White was demanding payment in full right now. David was more fearful now than ever before. Attorney Knight didn't know the half of it. David felt he had to do something to cover this mess, and do it fast. This extortion and blackmail against Johnson White had gone on for years. White had reached his limits and wasn't going to meet any more of David's demands. White had finally had enough and was ready to fight for his freedom.

David stayed in Nashville two days before driving back to Memphis. Late that night he arrived home, furious. Jenny was sleeping. He immediately woke her from her sleep.

"Jenny, Jenny, Wake up." David said, shaking Jenny vigorously. *"We have to talk. Wake up."*

"What's wrong, honey?" Jenny asked, as she sat up in the bed.

David sat on the bed beside Jenny to inform her of what had happened. *"White wants out."* David said. *"He's not going to give us another dime. He has hired Matthew Middleton as his go-between boy because he doesn't have the balls to confront me himself. Matthew put a freeze on our assets and is demanding that I pay White two million dollars right now!" That no-good black bastard, I never did like his ass.*

"Are you serious?" Jenny sounded shocked.

"Hell yes, I'm serious. And I believe Matt's dead serious too."

"White can't do that," Jenny said. *"All the money he has given us is entered in on our records as donations."*

"Donations," David shouted! *"Be real Jenny. What jury is going to believe a White man is just donating thousands and thousands of dollars to a Black man's business year after year? That's crazy."*

Jenny moved closer to David to comfort him. *"We can fight this Honey. It's his word against ours."*

David blurted out in anger again! *"Don't be a fool Jenny, his word against ours! White has all the evidence in the world against us! And if that damn Matthew brings this case up to that stupid ass friend of yours she'll tell him everything she knows; and blow the fucking lid off my shit. Damn Jenny, we have to do something now, and fast!"*

"Ann doesn't know everything," Jenny explained. *"I have never talked to her about anything."*

"She's the only eyewitness against us, David shouted! *She knows enough to send my ass to jail for life, and yours too! All it'll take is some small time attorney like Matthew, trying to make a name for himself, to bring my whole empire down. And Ann is the only person who can help him do it. We have to get rid of her ass, and fast, too."*

"What do you mean, get rid of her ass?" Jenny shouted.

"Hell, I don't know;" David shouted, *"anything! Tamper with the damn brakes on that cheap ass car she drives. Put something in her damn food and poison her ass. I don't know!"* David stood up and started pacing back and forth.

"Are you crazy?" Jenny shouted. *"Are you asking me to do something stupid like that? Don't be stupid David; you know I can't do anything crazy like that. Doing harm to Ann is like doing harm to my own flesh and blood."*

"Your own flesh and blood," David shouted back at Jenny! *"What in the hell are you talking about; what am I Jenny? What am I? Am I your own flesh and blood? Do you want your own flesh and blood to go to jail for thirty or forty years; the father of your own children? What else in the hell can we do? It's her or me, Jenny. It's up to you! I never liked that black Bitch anyway. I knew she was going to be a thorn in my side the very first time I saw her black ass. All she has ever done is snoop around and stay in our business. She has never been any use for anything. She's just a useless, impractical Bitch, just hanging around sucking up somebody else's joy. I say, get rid of her ass! And, Jenny,"* David hollered, pointing his finger at Jenny, *"you keep that Bitch the hell away from my children!"* David then went across the hall to the guest bedroom, slammed the door, and got in the bed.

Chapter 12

The price we pay for our mistakes

Weeks passed and the coldness of winter was overcome by the birth of the early stages of spring. But every moment of Jenny and David's world was being haunted by unpleasant occurrences that happened in their past. They were both nervous wrecks. Jenny could hardly sleep, and every time David was home, they quarreled about Ann.

David spent many hours, several days, combing through bogus evidence he hoped would prove Johnson White drugged a young Black female college student in his home and raped her. David wanted to prove that this same student became pregnant from this rape, and miscarried, without involving Jenny or himself. He also wanted to produce an eyewitness who would testify in a court of law that White committed this heinous crime without involving Jenny. This entire ordeal was mindboggling for David; causing him to be emotionally overwhelmed, coupled with uncontrollable anger and fear.

On the other hand, Johnson White, a multi-millionaire, could be ruined for life if this malicious act was dragged out in court. He could lose his wife, his children and possibly millions of dollars in revenue. For years, David had held this "one night affair" over Johnson White's head, blackmailing him out of thousands of dollars to enhance the quality of his pharmaceutical business. So far, all of David's great ideas had worked, netting him many hundreds of thousands of dollars in returns. Many doctors prescribed medications for hundreds of patients, daily, from David's corporation. Drugstores on every corner stocked his products and equipment. David had created a world of unlimited wealth and now, finally, after years of success, his empire was about to come tumbling down. He believed getting rid of Ann was the only way to save it. He and Jenny quarreled constantly.

"David, what are you;" Jenny shouted. *"How can you be so evil and unkind? I have been by your side from the first day we met, supporting you, helping you, covering up all your shit! For God's sake David, how can you want me to commit such a cold-hearted act! I'm the mother of your children!"*

"Do you want our lives to be unfolded in a fucking courtroom?" David shouted! *"Do you want me to go to jail? Is that what you want Jenny? Ann was there Jenny! Pot committed a crime when she aborted that baby. And Ann is the only person who knows you removed the embryo and placenta from their dorm room and delivered it to me at General. Then I'll have to tell how you took thousands of dollars from incapable interns for the key to medical exams they never would have passed. How you have flown to and from Mexico, India, and Thailand, transporting illegal drugs to abort fetuses for your rich and famous friends. How you supplied your phony doctor friends with illegal cocktails to aid them in their sexual fantasies! And all those other things you don't want anyone to know about!"* David was angry and sweating as he tried to coerce Jenny into seeing it his way.

"You would do that to me, wouldn't you?" Jenny said, in a soft and hurtful tone.

"You can bet your damn life I would!" David whispered.

David looked at Jenny with anger in his eyes and left the room. All that pressure from David was wear and tear on Jenny. She tried to convince him that they had nothing to worry about, but he wouldn't hear it. He pressured her to no end.

For many days, Jenny tried to avoid Ann as much as possible. Most of the time, she wouldn't accept Ann's telephone calls. Ann didn't know what to make of it, so she decided to pay Jenny a visit. Ann thought Jenny may be avoiding her because she may be pregnant again. Ann arrived at Jenny and David's home and Harriet, the housekeeper, answered the door.

"Ms. Ann, how are you?" Harriet greeted Ann.

"Hi Harriet, I'm fine:" I replied. *"Is Jenny home?"*

"Yes. Come in. Have a seat in the study. I'll let Mrs. Jamieson know you're here."

Ann waited in the study, admiring the beautiful paintings and art work. Finally, Jenny entered the room.

"Jenny." I said, as I hugged her. *"What's going on? Why haven't you returned my telephone calls?"*

"I've been very busy" Jenny responded. *'And on top of that, I haven't been feeling well at all."*

"Well, why don't you go to the doctor?" I said.

"Go to the doctor, are you serious? Don't be silly Ann. I'll be okay. I just need something to help me sleep."

"You need something to help you sleep! You're not sleeping?"

"I'm sleeping Ann," Jenny explained. *"But I'm a little restless. But I'll be okay."*

"Is all this restlessness and problems sleeping happening because you're pregnant again?"

"No Ann," Jenny shouted. *"I'm not pregnant again! I just want to be left alone! I want some time to myself. Can't you understand that?"*

"Okay, yes," I said, feeling a little hurt after Jenny shouted at me. *"I understand. You have my telephone number. When you have had enough time to yourself, give me a call."*

Ann left Jenny's home, got into her car, and drove away. Jenny peered at Ann from a window in the study as Ann drove off. Ann was confused. She didn't know what to think, but she did know that something was wrong. As soon as Ann got home she telephoned Pot. Pot answered her telephone.

"Pot, hey;" I said to Pot. *"I think you need to come home."*

"What!" Pot shouted. *"Come home! Come home for what?"*

"Jenny is talking crazy" I said. *"And I don't know what's wrong with her. She's sounding strange."*

"Sounding strange; Pot laughed. *"That's nothing new. Jenny has always sounded strange. She has always looked strange and is always doing strange things. You know she's not dealing with a full deck. And I can't just up and come home at the drop of a hat. I'm halfway around the world, not right down the street."*

"But I've never known her to act this weird." I said. *"And when I visited her today she smelled of alcohol and she wouldn't look at me. She wouldn't make eye contact with me at all. I'm serious Pot. This is very unusual"*

"I'm serious too." Pot said. *"Jenny's all right. You know she has two exceptionally intelligent children. That's a handful, plus, that crazy, deranged, wacko husband she never should have married. I'm surprised she hadn't tried to fly across the sky as a dodo bird."* Pot laughed out loud as she said: *"I was just kidding. But stop worrying so much Ann, everything is okay."*

"Okay." I said, as I laughed at Pot. *"Maybe I'm overreacting. Maybe it's nothing. I guess I've been eating too much chicken or something."*

Pot, laughing out loud again, replied, *"Eating too much chicken! You're in that big beautiful house all by yourself. And all you've got to do is eat chicken? You better call Allen Fulton over and have yourself some sex! Do something nice for yourself for a change Ann, and stop worrying about everybody else. Call Allen over and keep his ass all night!"*

"You are so crazy." I said, laughing too. *"Go ahead and have a nice time Pot. I'll see you when you get back."*

"Okay. Love you Ann. Bye."

"Love you too Pot; goodbye."

****

Ann took Pot's advise and went about her own business, hoping everyday that Jenny may call. Several days passed and

still, no call from Jenny. However, doing this same time, Ann's name rang out loud, in the Jamieson's household, every time Jenny and David were home alone. David believed Ann was the only person standing between him and his going to jail. He constantly thought about Ann being there when Jenny brought Pot's soiled clothes, the fetus, and Pot's placenta to him at General Hospital. David believed if he got rid of Ann, he had a good chance of winning if Matthew took him to court. This was an enormous amount of weight on David's shoulders. He was weary, worn and more stressed now than ever before. His madness was irrepressible and he pressured Jenny constantly, trying to get her to see it his way.

"I'm telling you, Jenny," David shouted, *"If we get rid of Ann, we can win this thing! She's the only person standing in our way!"*

"But you're asking me to harm someone I love." Jenny yelled! *"Why can't you understand that?"*

"Is that to say you don't love me," David bellowed in anger; *"and you don't love your children? How can you love her and not love us! I guess you feel about us, the same way your real parents felt about you. I guess you want to abandon us like your real parents abandoned you!"*

"What do you want David?" Jenny shouted, at wit's end, beginning to doubt her own sanity. *"Okay David! Okay! What in the hell do you want me to do? Tell me! I can't take this anymore!"*

David walked over to Jenny; held her tight in his arms, and whispered softly to her. He was happy he had finally won her over.

"We have to do this Honey." David whispered. *"You'll see. Once it's all over and things are back to normal, we'll be happy again. All this madness will be behind us. This is something we have to do Honey! Believe me, everything will be okay."*

David had a plan and finally, Jenny was ready to listen. He told Jenny he would send everyone away on a short trip; leaving the two of them home alone. David said he would be called away on an urgent business affair in Nashville. He said he would leave the front door unlocked and slightly open. Ann comes over, it's dark, she finds the front door slightly open, comes inside, and Jenny, being home alone, hears something down stairs and becomes afraid. Jenny thinking it may be a prowler, gets the gun, see someone coming up the stairs and fires, accidentally shooting Ann. David had it all planned and talked Jenny into going along with this evil act of violence.

****

The time came and everything was going as David planned. The kids and the nanny were off for a couple days at Disney. David drove them to the airport himself. He wanted to be sure they were gone. Jenny waited quietly at home, getting wasted on gin and tonic. When David returned from the airport, he drilled her several times, over and over again, on what he needed her to do. He made sure the lights were out inside the house and outside the house; leaving a small lamp on in their bedroom. Shortly after David left for Nashville, Jenny telephoned Ann. Ann was happy and elated to hear from her.

"Ann, Hi; it's me, Jenny."

"Jenny. I'm so glad you called! I've been waiting for you to call every day."

I was happy Jenny called, but I could feel something was wrong. Jenny sounded as if she had been crying, and she sounded intoxicated.

"I want to apologize for my inexcusable behavior the day you came over." Jenny said. *"I was being my old stupid self! You know I can be an ass sometimes."*

"No Jenny, you're not stupid and you're not an ass. You just needed some space. We all need space at sometimes or another. And I can understand that. I'm just so happy you decided to call. Are you okay? Have you been drinking?"

"Yes Ann. I have been drinking. And I'm going to continue to drink! Drinking is good for me. It helps me think and sort things out in my mind."

"Where's David Jenny?" I asked, being concerned about Jenny's drinking. She could never hold her liquor. A few hits of gin and tonic and Jenny was intoxicated.

"Hell, I don't know;" Jenny said. *"And right now, I don't give a damn."*

"Where are the children, Jenny?" I ask.

"They're all gone; all of them. And right now, I don't want to talk about David. I don't want to talk about the kids. I want to talk about us. You, me, and Pot, okay! I want you to listen and I want you to listen real good."

"Okay Jenny," I said. *"Sure, I'm listening."*

Ann was becoming very concerned. Jenny sounded as if she had been drinking much too much. Ann was concerned about Jenny being home alone. She didn't want Jenny to stagger and fall and injury herself.

"Ann," Jenny said. *"I have been a fool. I have always turned my back on you and Pot for David. And I still do crazy things! Sometimes I don't know what the hell is wrong with me! I let David use me and I let him use you and Pot too."*

"No Jenny." I said. *"That's not true and you know it. That's not true and I don't want to hear you say ugly things like that."*

"Listen to me Ann, listen to me!" Jenny shouted! *"Oh yes, it's true! But, I would always keep quiet about it. I didn't want to lose David. I did everything I could to hold on to him. I just wanted a man in my life! David never really loved me. I know that now. He used me, and everyone else, and I let him do it*! (Jenny started to cry as she continued to talk.)

"I stood by and let David drug Pot and give her, and Johnson White, some kind of potent potion so Johnson could have sex with her, and I never said a word! I saw David put the stuff in their drinks Ann; and I didn't even try to stop him! I can't forgive myself for that. The only two people, in this world, who truly love me and I betrayed y'all."

"But Jenny," I said. *"You didn't know David was a person like that. You loved him then and you love him now."*

"You bet I loved him! You don't know the half of it Ann! I would lie, steal, and cheat for him. Where do you think all our money came from? Doctors don't earn a million dollars a year! That money came from RU-486, Heroin, Barbs, LSD, Coke, you name it Ann, and David could get it for you. All he

had to do was make a few telephone calls and his shit was done. But he's smart Ann, he's smart. He never gets his own hands dirty; he always gets someone else to do his dirty work. Someone stupid, like me, and I hate myself for that!

"Jenny, please." I said. *"I don't want to know stuff like that. You've been drinking too much."*

"Me? Drinking too much? I'm not drunk. I'm a dirty bitch and I hate myself for it! I stood by and let David give Pot a hysterectomy, and I did nothing. He wanted Pot and I knew it! He knew she wouldn't have him so he fixed her, hoping no other man would want her. And I stood by and let him do it! Oh, Ann. I'm so ashamed!"

"Jenny, listen to me," I said. *"There was nothing you could do about that! I was there and there was nothing you could do! I'm coming over Jenny. I'm coming over right now! You need someone with you. You don't need to be alone. I'm coming right now Jenny."*

Ann immediately hung up the telephone and rushed to her car. Ann was feeling worried and nervous. She thought Jenny was having a nervous breakdown and going out of her mind. She drove to Jenny's home as fast as she could. She knew Jenny really needed her. She had to get there fast!

All that time, Jenny was holding a revolver in her hand. After hanging up the telephone, she staggered out of her bedroom and fell to the floor at the top of the stairs; sobbing and weeping; physically exhausted and emotionally drained. Between all the stress and all the alcohol, Jenny really needed professional medical care. By the time Ann arrived, Jenny was laying there, on the floor, at the top of the stairs, whimpering like a child.

When Ann arrived, Ann noticed the house was pitch, black dark. She slowly parked her car and made her way to Jenny's front door, carefully observing her surroundings. Ann noticed the front door was slightly ajar. So she slowly went inside, trying not to make a sound. Upon entering the house, she could hear Jenny whimpering. It sounded like Jenny was at the top of the stairs. The house was very dark, so Ann softly called out to Jenny.

"Jenny?" I called to Jenny in a soft and gentle manner. *"Jenny. Where are you? Are you okay?"*

Jenny yelled at Ann as if she was a raging mad woman. All that booze, stress, hurt, and pain, had caused Jenny to function as a mentally ill person.

"Ann," Jenny yelled*! "Don't come up here! I have a gun and I will kill you. Believe me Ann; I have a gun, and I will shoot you! You hear me? I will shoot you! I will kill you Ann!"*

Jenny sounded out of her mind and Ann wanted to help her. Ann stopped at the bottom of the stairs and talked to Jenny in a very soft, caring voice.

"Jenny." I said. *"Let me help you. Let me call someone to help you. It's okay. I'm here and I'm not going to leave you. We can get through this. It's no big deal. We have gone through things much worse than this. Let me help you Jenny. Please let me help you."*

"No!" Jenny screamed. *"I will shoot you Ann. I will shoot you dead! I don't want your help. So leave me the hell alone. Get the hell away from me. I'm warning you Ann, I will kill you. I will kill you! "*

As Jenny continued to scream at Ann in a very loud voice, Ann quickly flicked the lights on. And at that very moment, in a split second, Jenny stood up, raised the revolver above her head, and with both hands, started shooting toward the ceiling. As the bullets sounded, Ann became hysterical and SCREAMED a piercing cry, calling Jenny's name.

"JENNNNY!"

Somehow, at that very moment, as Ann screamed, the Spirit of God was awakened in Mama Sarah. Mama Sarah got out of bed, got on her knees, and began praying intensively!

"My dear Father God," Mama Sarah prayed. *"Something has happened. I can feel it in my Sprit and I don't feel good about it. Whatever it is, my Father, please, let it pass us by. If it's filled with heartache and sorrow, please, let it pass us by. Send your angels and our ancestors to protect us my Father. Let no evil come upon us. Rescue us! Hide us in your secret place and deliver us from all evil. You are our Father, our God, our refuge, our strength, our protector; Blesseth be your Holy Name! To you, my Father, my God, I give all the Praise and all the Glory, Forever and Forever!*

When the bullets were all gone from the gun, Jenny fell to the floor. Ann rushed to the top of the stairs to her. Blood was flowing from Jenny's head to the floor. Ann was hysterical, but somehow, she managed to get to the telephone and called the police.

Within minutes the police, ambulance, and news reporters arrived. Jenny was pronounced dead at the scene. The police investigated and ruled her death an accident. The police incident report stated that one of the bullets from the revolver, fired by the victim, hit a chandelier hanging from the ceiling, ricocheted and struck the victim in her head, killing her.

The police contacted Jenny's family and telephoned Mama Sarah. Mama Sarah immediately arrived with Kate and Big to pick Ann up. After speaking with the officer in charge, they immediately took Ann to the emergency room for a routine check, to make sure she was okay. Big trailed them, driving Ann's car. The ER doctor examined Ann, said she was okay, and discharged her with a mild sedative to help her sleep.

After leaving the hospital, they all went to Mama Sarah's house. Upon their arrival, Ann immediately telephoned Pot. Pot answered the telephone. At the sound of Pot's voice, Ann started to whimper and cry.

"Pot." I said, with tears rolling down my face. *"It's me, Ann.*

"Ann what's wrong? Why are you crying?"

"Oh, Pot! Something terrible has happened! It's Jenny. She's dead! She's dead Pot!"

"What!" Pot shouted. *"Jenny's dead, what are you saying Ann; what're you talking about, what happened?"*

"I don't know Pot! I don't know!" I said as I cried. *"She wasn't sounding good at all. So I went over to see what was*

wrong. She had a gun and started shooting everywhere! One of the bullets ricocheted and hit her."

"Oh my God Ann, Oh my God" Pot starts to cry.

"Please Pot, please don't cry." I said, as I cried too.

Mama Sarah took the phone from Ann and talked to Pot,

"Pot, it's me, Mama Sarah. Are you okay?" Mama Sarah asked Pot in a soft voice. *"Is someone there with you?"*

"Yes ma'am;" Pot said. *"I'm okay. My friend is here with me and I'll be home as soon as I can."*

"Okay, darling:" Mama Sarah said. *"If you need us baby, please call us back, okay? We love you Pot. We love you."*

"Yes ma'am; I Love y'all too. I'm on my way home now. Goodbye."

Pot hung up the phone and her sweetheart, who was right there by her side, heard every word that was said. He held Pot close to him to comfort her, and they immediately started making plans to return to Memphis. Mama Sarah and Kate medicated Ann and tucked her in for a restful night of sleep.

Deacon Johns and Ms. Linda had all ready arrived at Jenny's home. They were driving up when Mama Sarah and Kate were leaving with Ann.

David returned home, wondering what in the hell went wrong. He then called for the children to return home, unsure how to break this terrible news to them.

The next morning, Mama Sarah got up early to prepare breakfast. Ann and Kate slept a little late. Finally, Ann woke up, showered, and felt much better. After breakfast, it suddenly dawned on Ann that she needed to call and tell Matthew.

Ann telephoned Matthew at his apartment. A woman answered the telephone. Matthew was coming out of the shower when the phone rang.

"Hello" the woman answered.

"Yes, this is Ann Foster," I said to the woman. *"Is this Matthew Middleton's residence?"*

"Yes, it is." The woman said.

"May I speak to him please" I was totally bewildered and baffled about a woman answering Matthew's telephone.

"He's in the middle of something important at the moment. Can you hold on?"

"Sure." I said to the woman. *"Thank you."*

Matthew was walking into the room with a towel wrapped around his waist; refreshed and energized after his shower. The woman was holding the telephone. She gestured to him that the party was holding for him. Thinking it may not be important, he took his time to answer.

"Yes, this is Matthew, who's this." Matthew asked.

213

"Matthew." I said. *"It's me, Ann."*

Ann's voice trembled. She couldn't say another word. She started to cry and hung up the telephone.

"Ann! Ann!" Matthew called. *"Hello! Ann. Hello!"*

Realizing Ann had hung up the telephone; Matthew dialed her right back. Ann picked up the telephone, held it for a moment, hung it up, and silenced the ringer. Matthew tried calling back several times, over and over again, but no one answered. For the next few days, he telephoned Ann every few minutes, but no one answered. Matthew was a wreck. It was very difficult for him to concentrate and focus at work. And after hearing about Jenny's tragic accident, he was highly disturbed. Matthew rescheduled all his appointments and booked the next flight out to Memphis. He vowed to himself; if he got Ann back, he would never let her go!

****

Deacon Johns and David arranged Jenny's services so fast! Family and friends from other cities had to rush to Memphis to be in attendance at the funeral. Her services were three days after her demise. Ann hoped and prayed that Pot would get there in time. Finally, Pot arrived at the burial site. Ann was so relieved and so pleased.

After the burial, sadness came over the whole neighborhood. It rained and everyone went their separate ways. David took the children home. Deacon Johns and Ms. Linda went home. Pot went home with Polly Mae and Robert Lowell to spend some time with them and Ann went home with Mama Sarah. A few hours later, Amy Mae and Charlie Murphy headed back to Detroit; Charlie Murphy had to be back at work the following Monday morning. Kate and Big left the next morning for a much needed vacation they had planned a year before.

Ann was sad to see everyone leave, but she needed this time to spend with Mama Sarah. She needed to sort out her thoughts and try to understand how all this happened. Ann stayed at Mama Sarah's two days. She slept in the bed right behind Mama Sarah as she did when she was a child. They lounged around during the day, spending most of their time just talking. They popped popcorn and oiled the scalp of each other's hair.

"Mama," I called to Mama Sarah. *"You want some more of this popcorn?"*

"Naw Baby," Mama Sarah said. *"I've already eaten too much. Help yourself. Get you some and come on so I can finish oiling your hair."*

Ann returned to the family room, eating popcorn, and sat on the floor in front of Mama Sarah so she could finish Ann's hair. They talked about everything. Ann pouring her heart out to Mama Sarah was like a good session with a well trained psychotherapist. Ann needed to talk about Jenny's accident. She needed to overcome her pain and heal. And Mama Sarah

was ready to help Ann find comfort and joy amidst all her grief.

"Mama," I said in a very soft tone. *"I'm hurting so bad. Every time I close my eyes I can see Jenny. I keep praying, asking God to give me strength to get through this. But it's so hard."*

"My darling baby," Mama Sarah said to Ann. *"I know this is hard for you, but, you must keep thinking in your mind and speaking these words: "This too shall pass, this too shall pass." Keep speaking these words out of your mouth and believe them with all your heart and it will pass. This too shall pass."*

"But Mama, I knew something was going on with Jenny. If she would have talked to me, I believe I could have helped her."

"Hush, child." Mama Sarah said. *"Don't blame yourself. You've got to rest in the Lord. Have faith to move on and live. Don't look to the past, look to the goodness of a better tomorrow. Life is good, and God wants us to be happy and enjoy all these wonderful gifts He has given us on this beautiful earth. God wants us to have lots of laughter and happiness in our lives. When your Poppa Jack died, I almost lost my mind. God had to work hard to save me. God knew I needed to be here for you. So think on good things so you'll be here for your grandchildren and great grandchildren. Whenever bad or sad thoughts come into your mind, change them immediately and think of something good. Always think good thoughts, always speak kind, happy words, and always do good deeds. Make the Lord proud."*

"Oh Mama," I said. *"You are so good. You're a comfort to my soul. I thank God every day for having you in my life. You are a blessing to me. I'm going to visit David the first thing*

tomorrow morning and talk to him. I'm going to ask if he needs my help with Lizzie and DJ and spend as much time as I can to help him with those children. I want to be there for them."

"Sure, baby." Mama Sarah said. *"That's a good thing to do. Those children need you and Pot too. I think the two of you are exactly what they all need."*

Ann slept well that night. She woke the next morning refreshed and even sang in the shower. Mama Sarah laughed as she listened to Ann sing. She was pleased to hear Ann's happy Spirit again. Ann dressed, had coffee with Mama Sarah and was off to David's house. When she arrived, the sadness of Jenny's death came upon her, but she immediately removed it from her mind and made her way to the front door. Thinking of all the good things she wanted to do. She rang the doorbell and was startled, Deacon Johns answered the door.

"What are you here for Heifer?" Deacon Johns shouted. *"To kill Jenny's husband, and children like you killed her? Well, you backstabbing darkie, they ain't here! All of them are gone! Gone to Boston, where I hope they will stay, to be away from rats like you and that half-baked grand mammy of yours!"*

Ann stood there in a state of shock. Her hands were shaking, covering the lower half of her face. Tears started to roll down her face like raindrops. Deacon Johns continued to raise his voice, shouting at her in anger!

"Go ahead, you slut. Cry! Cry your damn eyes out you bitch."
"But you remember, it shouldn't be Virginia laying out there

in that grave yard, it should be your black ass and that wildcat harlot you're shacking up with!"

Ann was emotionally scorned. She couldn't say a word. She turned and ran to her car, mentally wounded with pain and drove away. Ann cried so hard. She didn't stop driving until she was home. Ann sat in her car several minutes, crying desperately, unsure of what to do. Finally, she pulled herself together, dried her eyes, and went inside the house. Pot's car was parked outside. Ann called to Pot as she entered the house.

"Pot, Pot," I called to Pot. *"Are you home?"*

"I'm in here." Pot answered.

Ann walked into the room where Pot was. Pot was packing a suitcase.

"Where're you going?" I asked.

"I'm leaving," Pot said.

"Leaving?" I said. *"You were going to leave without telling me?"*

"Yes Ann, I was." Pot said. *"Stop clinging to me Ann, because I'm sure going to stop clinging to you."*

"Stop clinging to you" I shouted! *"What do you mean by that? You're my family! We can't leave Jenny hanging like this. We have to find out what happened to her and find where David has taken those children. We have to get them back!"* (Tears started to trickle down Ann's face.)

218

"Get them back?" Pot shouted. *"Aren't you tired of fighting Ann? Let go, Ann! Let go! Our lives have been one big mess after another. I need to be free! You can stay here and free the damn ghetto, and love everybody, and rescue Jenny's children! I'm getting the hell away from this damn fuckin' place!"*

This anger in Pot had built up over many years! Ann stood there listening, sniffing, and fighting back her tears as she listened. Pot continued in anger. Pot was so angry and hurt she couldn't take it any more. She had to get away. Pot continued to talk as she prepared to leave.

"As Black people we have so much to be grateful for," Pot said. *"But what do we do; we always act a damn fool! We despise each other and treat each other like shit! All we think about is whose dark skinned, whose light skinned! Is she pregnant? Is that her hair? I don't like her, she don't like me. There's no way we can be successful among stupid people like that! It's self hate Ann; it's self hate! We fight, stab, and shoot each other. And all rich Black folk do, is prey on poor Black folk. You know as well as I do, that David was behind Jenny's death. I know he had something to do with it! He has used all of us. You, me, and everybody he can make a fool of! And all we do is look stupid and let it happen. Why can't we love one another? What's wrong with us? I just want to get as far away from ignorant Black folk as I can. I don't care if I never come back!"*

"But Pot." I said. *"Let's sit down. You're just mad. Let's sit down and figure this thing out. There has to be an answer."*

219

"Figure this thing out!" Pot shouted. *"What in the hell are you talking about Ann, we're not God! But if you want to continue with misery and unhappiness in your life, be my guest. You figure this shit out! I'm leaving!"*

Pot took her luggage to her car. Ann walked right behind her, trying to convince Pot to stay. Pot got in her car and started to drive off. Ann jumped in the car with Pot, crying, and begging Pot not to go. Pot continued driving.

"Pot, please don't go!" I cried. *"This is not a good time. We can get through this! Please, Pot. Don't go."*

Pot continued driving, speaking from her heart. Pot was very angry and very broken!

"Jenny was such a good person." Pot said. *"Her whole life was lived, trying to make this world a better place for us. For us Ann, Black people! And what thanks did she get? None! If it wasn't for me, you and her kids, she wouldn't have had any love at all. From a child, and all through her adulthood, I saw people hate Jenny! Her own family, her husband, people in our neighborhood, the kids at school, her in-laws! These are not White people, Ann. These are Black people. And you want to know why? It's because they are stupid, ignorant, and don't give a damn! And you want me to figure it out!"*

Ann and Pot arrived at the airport. Pot had her luggage checked and gave the valet the card to park her car. Ann followed right behind Pot, still trying to convince Pot not to go.

People were staring at them, wondering what the hell was going on. Ann was still crying.

"Pot, please don't go?" I cried. *I don't know what to do. I'm almost out of my mind! I need you to help me Pot! I need you to help me get through this. Tell me what to do? Tell me where you're going? When will you be coming back?"*

"Leave, Ann. Leave this place!" Pot shouted, with tears rolling down her face. *"There's more to life than hurt and pain. And I'm going with my man Ann. Where, I don't know, but wherever we go, I hope he never bring me back to this damn place. And if you have any sense, you'll get the hell away from here too. There's nothing here for us Ann! Nothing! Can't you see that?"*

Pot hugged Ann, pulled away, and boarded her sweetheart's plane. He was standing at the plane's entrance door, waiting for Pot.

It was so very sad for both of them. With her face pressed against the window at the airport, Ann continued to cry. She stood at the window, tears running down her face, watching Pot board the plane. Pot, looking back at Ann, continued to cry too. The plane took off.

Ann was drained and weak. All she could do was sit there with tears running down her face. She felt in her heart that Pot had to come back. Pot's roots were here. She had to come back!

With Jenny gone, and now Pot had left, Ann was so overcome with hurt and pain, all she could do was cry. She sat there, for a moment, in the airport weeping desperately. Finally, she struggled to pull herself together to move on. She looked up,

and there, walking towards her was Matthew, staring at her and feeling her pain. He walked over to Ann, helped her to her feet, put his arms round her and held her close. Matthew looked at Ann and as Ann stared into Matthew's eyes, Ann knew for sure, at that very moment, that Matthew was the one. He was the one. It was all, right there, in his eyes.

God Bless

THE AUTHOR

Julice Howard Franklin

Julice Howard Franklin, the youngest of eight children, was born to her parents, Lee Andrew and Bertha Howard, in Holly Springs, Mississippi. At the age of three months old, her parents moved her to Memphis, Tennessee. Living in Memphis, Julice attended Manassas and Booker T. Washington High School and graduated college, earning a Bachelor's Degree from Memphis State University, now the University of Memphis.

Julice discovered her passion for writing as an adolescent, loving to write short stories and poems. Her first noted writing, "Stories Forever to Be Told" was an unpublished work of the history and chronology of her family and ancestors. As a college student, Julice wrote, developed and coordinated "Youth Exploring Career Goals" a career development program for young men age 12 to 15 years old.

During her employment for the State of Tennessee, Julice served as a Human Services Case Worker, a Juvenile Court Child Support Hearing Referee and an Educator for the Memphis and Shelby County Public School System. She served in the National Service of Americorps, and marched with Dr. Martin Luther King Jr. during his presence in Memphis to support the striking sanitation workers.

Aside from her passion for writing, Julice loves to do many things. She adores the gifts of nature and enjoys the beauty of the beautiful outdoors. She loves to listen to raindrops fall, and to all things peaceful, tranquil and calm. She loves a warm cup of tea while watching snow flakes fall from our beautiful sky. She is a mother, a grandmother, a great grandmother, and has the highest value of Love, Honor and Respect for the Grace and Power of our Great Creator.